Blaze™

Dear Reader,

I hope that you're enjoying my CHICKS IN CHARGE series. If you missed the first two books, please be sure to check them out. (*Getting It!* Harlequin Temptation January 2005 and *Getting It Good!* Harlequin Blaze February 2005). I've had a ball writing these feisty heroines and finding the perfect guys for them.

Since the debut book I've been asked many times where I got the idea for this series. It was funny, really. I was sitting in my office, absently listening to a panel of "experts" talk about why *The Bachelorette* had been more of a success than *The Bachelor*. One of the women shrugged and said, "It's because a chick's in charge." Something about the girl power in that phrase really appealed to me and I started playing the "What if…" game. The result was this series of books with smart, determined women who know their own worth. Pairing them with guys who figure it out as well has been a very fun and fulfilling experience.

Don't miss the final book in my CHICKS IN CHARGE series—*Getting It Now!*—available next month. I'd love to know what you think. Be sure to swing by my Web site— www.booksbyRhondaNelson.com and let me know how you're enjoying the ride.

Happy reading!

Rhonda Nelson

GETTING IT RIGHT!

Rhonda Nelson

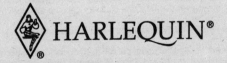

TORONTO • NEW YORK • LONDON
AMSTERDAM • PARIS • SYDNEY • HAMBURG
STOCKHOLM • ATHENS • TOKYO • MILAN • MADRID
PRAGUE • WARSAW • BUDAPEST • AUCKLAND

This book is dedicated to one of the nicest people
I have ever known, my good friend Pam Farris. PTO,
sons and daughters, Girl Scouts, midnight movies, countless
lunches, hair days and pool days, your unfailing friendship
has been a source of great joy for me
over the years and I look forward to many more.

ISBN 0-373-79221-2

GETTING IT RIGHT!

www.eHarlequin.com

Printed in U.S.A.

Prologue

UNDER ORDINARY circumstances, April Wilson was just vain enough to appreciate a hot stare from an equally hot guy. What woman didn't like a lingering appreciative look? One that somehow managed to validate those extra minutes spent in front of the mirror, that additional time rifling through the closet to find *the* perfect outfit, or taking those few seconds to repair a chipped nail?

Usually one flicker of interest from a pair of intrigued masculine eyes was enough to make her inwardly preen with satisfaction because it meant she hadn't wasted her time, that her somewhat manic attention to detail had paid off.

Unfortunately, in this case, it was the particular *source* of interest that was causing her...discomfort.

Looking equally relaxed and dangerous, Ben Hayes sat sprawled on a chair at the end of the bar.

The Blue Monkey Pub on the edge of New Orleans' famed French Quarter was technically *her* haunt, but over the past few months Ben had been showing up with disconcerting regularity and had easily made it his preferred hang out, as well. It was unnerving to say the least. Her gaze was inexplicably drawn to him once more, causing a flutter of awareness to skim up her spine.

Mercy.

A navy-blue designer T-shirt clung to his broad shoulders and muscled chest, serving as both a testament to his casual style and the pricey label, a silent affirmation that he'd arrived. April swallowed.

That, she knew, was important to him.

Worn denim clung to his hardened thighs and a pair of ridiculously expensive boots rounded out the ensemble. Dark brown hair just a shade shy of black hung in loose waves around a face that held more character than beauty and, though she couldn't see them clearly from here—*and* she refused to look—memory painted an accurate picture of his eyes. Pale golden brown, the shade of light arcing off a crystal tumbler of good Kentucky bourbon.

Occasionally he'd hoist the longneck held carelessly between his fingers to that insanely carnal mouth and, though she seriously doubted he was even aware of it, every move he made exuded an effortless, sexy sort of grace that was essentially mesmerizing to every female—attached and un-attached—in the room.

Simply put, Ben Hayes was sex on a stick…and from the time she was old enough to feel the first quickening of awareness in her belly, licking him all over had been a fantasy she'd explored repeat-edly in her dreams.

Frankie Salvaterra—soon to be Hartford, April reminded herself—and a fellow Chicks In Charge buddy, leaned over and nudged her shoulder. Her dark brown eyes glittered with perception and just the smallest hint of pity. "It's getting to you, isn't it?"

"What?" April asked, knowing full well what her friend meant. When it came to sexual matters, as CHiC's Carnal Contessa, Frankie was the go-to girl for advice.

"That stare." She cocked her head toward the bar. "Ben's been boring a hole through you for the past fifteen minutes." Her lips curled. "My guess is that he's mentally stripped you naked and committed carnal acts upon your person on every available. surface in this room, ones that would undoubtedly end your *suffering*," she said, needling April significantly, then sipped her drink and sighed. "If only you'd let him."

April closed her eyes and let go a shuddering breath as Frankie's graphic description too readily materialized behind her lids. Her friend was right, she knew.

And she *was* suffering.

Without warning and for no apparent discernable reason, her Big O had vanished. Or at the very least headed for higher ground. For the past eighteen months—*eighteen miserable, excruciatingly frustrating months*—and despite multiple attempts, self-inflicted and otherwise, she'd been unable to climax. It was as though whatever tripped her trigger had been unwittingly put on safety.

At first, April had chalked her unhappy malady up to stress. With the creation of Chicks In Charge—a brainchild born in this very pub and an organization designed for the express purpose of empowering women everywhere—as the Webmistress of the movement, she'd been too busy to think about whether or not her hot button was disengaged.

Between building the original site, then pulling the CHiC e-zine together, not to mention maintaining sites for previous customers and working on prior contracted work, she'd been burning her candle at both ends.

Luckily, she was at her best under pressure and, though she was tired, it was the pleasant sort of exhaustion brought about by a job well-done. It was only in the past month when things had slowed to a more comfortable pace that the absence of a sex life and, more importantly, the melting pleasure of a hard, mind-numbing orgasm, had begun to wear on her.

And seeing Ben Hayes on a weekly basis—a six-and-a-half-foot, rock-hard and irreverent reminder of what she was missing—certainly wasn't helping matters. Hell, he wasn't dubbed *The Vagina Whisperer* for nothing, April thought with a small smile, wondering if he knew about the nickname.

Ben was a quintessential bad boy, a guy from the so-called wrong side of the tracks who thumbed his nose at the middle class, hated the idle rich and showed his disdain by competently seducing any girl he supposedly couldn't have, usually one already attached or engaged to a guy belonging to one of the aforementioned groups. He was a legendary lover, one of those fix-me males, and had left more than one broken heart in his wake…and, April thought as she took another sip of her beer, had her mother not intervened at a timely moment in her midteens, she would have undoubtedly ended up as one of them, as well.

"I know you said that Ben's father worked for your family while the two of you were growing up," Frankie said casually as the rest of the little group around their table continued to chat. "But to be honest, April, I've always suspected a deeper acquaintance. Something more than just child-hood friends."

As usual, Frankie's perceptive intuition was dead-on. They *had* been more than friends, at least until her mother had forbidden Ben to come near her. Funny thing, that, April thought now. Ben—her rebel—had been willing to fight for every-thing. Her lips twisted with bitter humor.

Everything, that is, except her.

Honestly, she'd never expected him to give in so easily. She'd been convinced of his affection, so certain of his love. Teenage fancy, she thought now. They hadn't been in love. She'd merely suf-fered from an extreme crush and he'd… Well, evidently, he'd just been horny. Furthermore, he'd changed after that encounter. Her good-hearted bad boy had become bewilderingly embittered. Angry, even.

"There was nothing more," April lied, the fib souring on her tongue. "We were friends. Our fathers served in Vietnam together. Ben's dad was injured while under my father's command, and couldn't keep steady work when they came home." She shrugged. "Dad hired him, gave his family a place to live."

Frankie quirked a dark brow. "He felt responsible then?"

April nodded. "Yeah. Still does, I think." He'd never told her why—and given the fact that she'd unwittingly forced him out of the closet a couple of years ago, their once-close relationship had become slightly…strained of late. April resisted the urge to roll her eyes. As if she cared about his sexual preference. She just wanted her father back.

Granted, having a father who was just as adept as she was at spotting a good-looking guy was a little unnerving, but in all honestly, after twenty years with her mother—The Great Emasculator—April was just glad that he'd found someone to make him happy. She only wished that her father would share that special someone with her.

Despite her attempts to wheedle an introduction, her father maddeningly continued to keep his companion's identity a secret. Her father was a good man, though, and deserved a bit of belated joy. As for her mother, well… She wouldn't go into what *she* deserved, April thought ominously.

"Why don't you just go talk to him?" Frankie said, once again bringing the subject back to Ben, or more accurately, April having sex with Ben.

April hesitated, then gave her head a small shake. "I don't think it's a good idea."

"And I think you're overthinking it." She shrugged. "He's obviously interested."

Yeah, *now,* April thought, after years of being distantly polite. It didn't make any sense. She briefly tuned into the conversation currently occupying the residents at their table. Zora and Tate were still arguing over who'd ultimately gotten Frankie and Ross together, and Carrie, the fourth and final member of their Chicks In Charge board, was looking on with an indulgent though tired smile.

Poor Carrie, April thought. She might have lost her orgasm, but Carrie was the only member of their little group who was still in a miserable job, beholden to a bastard employer. Carrie was a fantastic chef, though, and they were all convinced that good things were bound to be coming her way. In fact, the producers at *Let's Cook, New Orleans!*—a nationally syndicated program—were supposedly looking at their friend as a possible host and, in April's opinion, the show couldn't come soon enough.

Satisfied that she wasn't missing any new gossip, she summoned a wry smile and shifted against her bar stool. "We're supposed to be celebrating your impending nuptials, not worrying over my little problem," she said, hoping to change the subject. She knew Ben was the answer to her problem, she just wasn't looking forward to the conversation that would have to precede the cure.

Frankie shot a fond look at her husband-to-be. "Believe me, Ross and I have our own special brand of *celebrating*."

Unable to help herself, April grinned and determinedly ignored the prick of envy in her chest. She could just imagine. It was nice to see two of her best friends find their perfect mate. Zora and Tate had already tied the knot and Frankie and Ross weren't too far behind.

"And you don't have a *little* problem," Frankie continued doggedly. "After a year and a half, it's a big problem, babe." She cocked her head. "If Ben can't cure what ails you, then I think you need to seriously consider seeing a doctor. Something's not right. It's…" She frowned thoughtfully. "It's unnatural. Seriously. For the love of Mike, just go talk to him," Frankie ordered with an exaggerated huff. "What have you got to lose?"

Logic told her nothing, but intuition begged to differ. That's why she'd been dragging her heels and refused to seek out Ben's particular brand of expertise. Honestly, hearing about his sexual forays—and there'd been too many satisfied women singing his praises to avoid it—April grimly suspected even a casual encounter would cost her more than she could pay.

A beat slid into three, then Frankie arched a shrewd brow. "Oh, my," she said knowingly. "So it's like that."

April's beer stalled halfway to her mouth and she shot Frankie an annoyed look. "No it's not. There's nothing wrong with being cautious."

Frankie snorted. "You're beyond cautious. It's time to take the bull by the horns. Hell, even hot, sweaty sex without an orgasm is better than no sex at all, April." She chewed the corner of her bottom lip and grinned. "If nothing else, do him for the foreplay. His name has come up quite frequently in my line of work and from what I hear, Ben's got a master's in tongue massage."

And just like that, April cast Ben in the starring role of her own mental porn movie. *Warm hands and warmer skin, a hot greedy mouth...* Her thighs tensed and the slightest buzz of a tingle pinged her sex. And it was that little ray of hope that ultimately pushed her over the edge, conquered reason and thwarted doubt.

She *wanted.*

And she'd always wanted *him.*

"Go on," Frankie cajoled, evidently sensing victory. "Go talk to him."

"Fine," April finally relented. "But not tonight."

"But—"

"Not tonight," she repeated firmly. "What?" she said grimly under her breath. "You want me to walk up to him and tell him that I'm in need of some of his *whispering* skills?" She rolled her eyes. "Hardly. I need a plan first. I've got to have something to offer in return." What, she didn't know. Ben was a top-notch and well-paid photographer whose work had been featured in prominent glossies all over the globe. Money wasn't going to cut it. He didn't need it anymore.

Frankie's eyes bugged. "You mean sleeping with you isn't going to be payment enough? He wants you. *You* are what he gets."

"No," April said, lost in her own thoughts. "That's not how I want to handle this."

Frankie harrumphed and looked at her as though she'd grown a second head. "You're insane."

"Yeah, well, you try going without an orgasm for eighteen months and see how rational you are."

Her friend made a moue of understanding and conceded the point. "There is that." She paused. "But you are going to ask him for help, right? Promise me," she insisted.

April nodded and let go a pent-up breath. She sought Ben out once more and the hair on the back of her neck prickled when her gaze unexpectedly tangled with his. That hot, familiar stare and the faint crook of his ultra-sexy lips seemingly pinned her to her seat. Without warning, the air thinned in her lungs, her skin instantly warmed and tightened, and that woeful tingle below her navel issued another faint buzz of desperation.

"I promise," she said breathlessly.

And she secretly hoped like hell she didn't live to regret it.

1

"YOU'VE GOT A CALL on line one and a visitor in the parlor."

Ben Hayes wearily set the loupe aside he'd been using to study yesterday's negatives and rubbed his eyes. Shit, he thought as he leaned back in his chair. Complete and total shit. None of it even worth developing.

"Who's on the phone?"

Claudette's proud Cajun-French chin lifted into a stubborn, I-dare-you angle, one that Ben recognized all too well. It was reserved for one caller, in particular. "Your father."

Though he'd expected it, Ben felt himself tense, nonetheless, then had to force himself to relax. "Tell him I'm not here." His tone was flat, emotionless, and in no way hinted at the anger, hopelessness and regret that twisted his insides.

"Too late," his meddling secretary replied. "I've already told him you are."

"Then tell him I'm in a meeting."

Her thin nostrils flared as she pulled in a breath. Of patience, no doubt. Apparently running interference between him and his father was beginning to wear on her otherwise steely nerves. "He's already asked if you were in a meeting and I said no." The merest hint of a smile caught the corner of her compressed lips. "Looks like he's onto all of your excuses."

"Fine. You can tell him the truth." He shrugged. "Tell him I don't want to talk to him." Another lie. He'd love to talk to his father. Tell him how things were going. Basically shoot the shit and share a beer. Perks he knew other men enjoyed with their dads. But, despite his best attempts to get past the…complexities of his father's character, he simply couldn't do it. He'd tried…and he'd failed. And since failure was such an uncommon and unpleasant experience, he'd rather avoid it.

"Oh, for Pete's sake," Claudette finally snapped. "I'll tell him no such thing. He's your father. You should talk to him."

He did talk to him. On birthdays and holidays. "Claudette," he began warningly.

"Oh, fine," she begrudgingly relented. "I'll make up another excuse, tell the dear man another lie." She aimed a hard stare at him, one that seemed particularly intense considering she wore a tiny brooch with a picture of her beloved dog on her collar. "But this is the last time, Ben." She exhaled mightily. "Now what do you want me to do about the girl in the parlor? Tell her you're not in, as well?" she asked sarcastically.

Relief melted the tension out of his muscles, causing him to slouch back in his tufted leather chair. He arched a brow. "Depends," he said. "Who is she and what does she want?"

"Her name is April Wilson and, as for what she wants, you'll have to ask her yourself. She said it was personal."

Ben blinked, certain he'd misunderstood. "April Wilson?"

"Yes," Claudette replied cautiously, obviously sensing his surprise. "Do you know her?"

Ben felt a grim smile catch the corner of his mouth. Oh, yeah. He knew her. He could identify every freckle on her face, knew the exact curve of her brow, the varying shades of green that made up those wide expressive eyes of hers. He knew that purple was her favorite color, black-eyed Sus-

ans her favorite flower, and that when she was
nervous or tense, she had a tendency to chew the
corner of her plump bottom lip. He knew that she
liked to wear her hair up, that as a teenager she had
a huge crush on Rick Springfield and that she was
missing a nail on her left pinkie toe. A biking ac-
cident, if memory served, and admittedly, his
rarely failed where April was concerned.

In fact, he'd probably be a lot happier if it
would.

Despite years of separation and countless sub-
stitutes, despite time, distance, a complicated family history—*Ha!* he thought darkly—and more
sex than any man had a right to in a lifetime, April
Wilson still remained, and he grimly suspected
would *always* remain, the girl for him.

She'd unwittingly set the standard, and was the
one woman every other he'd crossed paths with
was compared to. For more than a decade he'd
been trying to recreate the magic, to find the same
sort of chemistry he'd had with her. The mind-
numbing, *soul-shattering* attraction that made a
man want to climb out of his own skin and into
hers.

He'd never found it.

Hell, he'd never even come close to capturing

that same sort of feeling, that awesome, unbeliev-able high. In fact, he'd all but convinced himself that it hadn't really existed, that his teenage über-hormones had somehow magnified and distorted the memory until it couldn't possibly be real.

But one chance meeting at the Blue Monkey Pub eighteen months ago had soon proved other-wise, and over the past year and a half, he'd made a concerted effort to be there on Friday nights just to look at her, share the same air, feel the buzz of her presence.

Pathetic, he knew, but he couldn't seem to help himself. Though he was no longer the green, eas-ily intimidated boy he'd been when her cruel bitch of a mother had banned him from her life, Ben had nevertheless resisted the almost overwhelming urge to seduce her. To see if she could still make the bottom drop out of his stomach with a mere smile.

He'd learned that she could, even when that smile wasn't directed at him.

Which was why, over the past couple of weeks, he'd been wrestling with the idea of seducing her anyway. Quite frankly, the idea of thumbing his nose at her parents—both of them, but for differ-ent reasons—was intensely appealing.

Her mother had robbed him of April, deemed him unworthy of her daughter. Ben smiled bitterly. Oh, but that hadn't been enough. She'd wanted to really wound him, to *really* hurt him and, as a result, she'd ultimately stolen his father, as well. Or at the very least, any respect he'd had for his dad. Until Morgana Wilson had spewed her poison, he'd enjoyed the ignorant bliss of thinking his father was perfect. The man had had problems, Ben knew. War had a way of ruining the best soldiers, and Davy Hayes had been no exception. But Ben had never doubted his father's character…until Morgana had taken that from him.

As for April's father… His lips twisted. Well, it was hard to pigeonhole his sins.

In the end, her parents had both directly and indirectly hurt him and, though he knew the best way to repay that sentiment would be to hurt their daughter, Ben had been unable to follow through. He wanted her more than he'd ever wanted anyone, but between the personal issues attached to her family and the taint of revenge attached to having her, he'd been unable to come to terms with the cost.

Both hers and his.

"Do you want me to send her in?" Claudette asked.

Still somewhat distracted, Ben nodded. Unfortunately, there was only one reason why April would come to see him—one he sure as hell wasn't interested in discussing—but he could hardly turn her away. It was April, after all, and just knowing that she was in the next room made his heart kick into an irregular rhythm.

With an expression of extreme curiosity Claudette gave him an odd look, then turned on her heel and walked out. Less than thirty seconds later she returned with April in tow, ushered her into the room, then with another blatantly interested look, once again made a reluctant exit.

If he'd had any manners at all, Ben would have stood when she came in, but for some reason his legs had turned to lead. Only years of pretending to be indifferent kept his mouth from breaking into a wide grin and fortunately the careless smile he'd mastered slid easily into place. Words momentarily failed him—he had absolutely no idea what to say—but in the end, he settled for a weak, "Er... This is a surprise."

April's small hand tightened around her purse strap and she cast an uneasy look around his office. "I hope I'm not intruding."

"Not at all." He finally found his feet and gestured toward a chair. "Please. Come sit."

Clad in a brown cable-knit sweater that ably hugged her curves and a pair of tailored cream wool slacks, April traveled the short distance to one of the walnut demi-marquise chairs that flanked his antique desk. Her mink curls were loose and tousled and the sting from the cold wind had colored her cheeks. A pair of diamond studs winked from her delicate lobes and the matching pendant lay nestled between her breasts, suspended from a fine gold chain. He caught the crisp scent of winter and the smallest whiff of jasmine as she settled into her seat.

As always, she looked chic, polished and approachable, a combination one didn't always see among those who were accustomed to money. Now that he moved within her circle, he could appreciate the difference.

She glanced around his office, her keen gaze inspecting a few of his more accomplished frames. "Beautiful work," she said softly. She gestured toward a sepia print behind his credenza. "Isn't that the staircase in the old Belle Fontaine mansion?"

Ben nodded. "It is."

In fact, it had been featured in *Southern Living*

last month. He started to tell her, but managed to just stop himself. He didn't have to validate his work, dammit—it spoke for itself.

Regardless, old habits died hard and while she'd never intentionally made him feel like the parasite poaching a living off her family the way her mother had, Ben nevertheless had a hard time shaking the need to showcase his own successes. Successes which had been hard-won, self-motivated and earned without so much as a favor from the Wilson family.

He'd take care of himself, by God. He'd be damned before he'd ever take a handout or become, as Morgana Wilson had so eloquently put it all those years ago, *another man's whore*. To this day he couldn't decide what was worse—learning that his father was gay, or realizing that the quiet gentle man he'd loved and respected had simply been too weak to support his family.

A prick of guilt for the uncharitable assessment surfaced, but Ben determinedly shook it off, squashed the happy memories that arose. As an adult he could appreciate another person's sexual orientation—he wasn't ashamed of his father for being gay. Unnerved? Yes. But not ashamed. He even understood that Vietnam had changed him—

could process, sort and compartmentalize every rational argument for the reasons his father had returned to American soil a little less stable than when he'd left.

But the one thing that Ben couldn't rationalize away, the one thing he couldn't let go of or forgive was the second-class citizenship his father had foisted upon his family by moving onto his lover's property. It cheapened his father and thereby, as far as he was concerned, lessened Ben's own value.

Since the moment he moved out of his father's house, *Ben* had set the standard for *his* self-worth and, while he missed his dad, being around him was a painful reminder of a past he could no longer be proud of. It was simply easier to avoid him. He didn't have to worry about avoiding his mother. She'd cut and run shortly after he'd asked her if Morgana's accusations were true. He hadn't heard from her since. God, he hated this, hated thinking about any of it.

"So," Ben said expectantly, both equally eager and reluctant to get this over with. "What can I do for you?"

It's not what you can do *for* me, but what you can do *to* me, April thought, silently agonizing over making the decision to come here.

What the hell had she been thinking? Why in God's name had she let Frankie talk her into this ridiculous plan? Yes, she desperately needed an orgasm, and yes, if there was any man capable of doing it for her on the planet, then it was the one sitting in front of her. Sweet mercy, but he was gorgeous. Every bit as perfect—and then some—as what she remembered. If Ben Hayes was sexy in the smoky low light of a semicrowded pub, it was nothing compared to the hot-factor he emitted in the natural morning luminance of his own element.

Creamy plaster walls, detailed oak molding and hardwood floors, heavy antiques dressed in rich fabrics and silky fringe, and beautiful framed artwork—his own, of course—rounded out a room that bespoke moneyed New Orleans style, mysterious, seductive and alluring. Seated behind a beautiful inlaid mahogany twin-pedestal desk, Ben looked every bit as mysterious, seductive and alluring as the city he called home. Even the sensual curve of his wicked mouth echoed the Big Easy's dark charm.

His almost-black hair was tousled, pushed carelessly away from his face and guarded golden eyes studied her with a calmness that was as arousing as it was unsettling. April let go of a shaky breath.

Quite honestly, she hadn't thought past coming here. If she had, she knew she would have never made the journey to his office, would have never found the nerve to cross his threshold. The question was, where the hell was she going to find the nerve to ask for his help? Or should she even ask for that matter? As Frankie had so keenly pointed out last week, he'd been staring a hole through her for months, silently seducing her with those mesmerizing heavy-lidded eyes. She smothered a snort. Short of marking his territory by peeing on her bar stool, he couldn't have possibly made his interest any more plain. And yet, here he sat, seemingly bemused by her presence.

Irritation surfaced and galvanized her. He wanted her, too, dammit. She needed to remember that. Rather than diving right into the heart of the matter, though, she decided to try a few pleasantries first. "Before we get to what you can do for me, tell me how you've been. I've seen you at the pub, but we haven't had a chance to talk."

A tactful lie. They could have talked at any time, if either one of them had made the move and, given the way they'd parted, she firmly believed *he* was the one who should have taken that step. It was a courtesy he owed her. After all, he'd broken her heart.

The small rebuke hit home, evidenced by the knowing twinkle in that too-perceptive gaze. Something about that familiar hint of humor made April marginally relax. She recognized this Ben. She'd known him. And she'd loved him with all the innocence held in her tender, teenage heart.

"You're always with your posse," he said, shrugging lazily. "I didn't want to intrude."

She chuckled. "My posse?"

"Yeah." He lifted a pen from his desk and tapped it thoughtfully upon the leather surface. "You know. Your *Chicks In Charge* friends."

So he'd kept up with her then, April thought, ridiculously heartened by that insightful little tidbit. "They wouldn't have minded."

His gaze caught and held hers. "I'll keep that in mind next time."

April nodded and moved on to another topic. "So…how's your dad doing?"

A shadow moved across his face and for a split second, he became unnaturally still. On guard, she realized, intrigued. He tossed the pen aside. "Fine, I suppose," he said, watching her closely. "I haven't spoken with him recently. How's yours?"

"The same." She shifted and looked away. "I,

uh… I haven't spoken to my father recently, either."

But not for lack of trying, she didn't add. Most of her calls were avoided and rarely returned. A part of her longed to confide in Ben, to tell him about accidentally outing her father, but the time for that had passed. They hadn't shared a secret in years. Odd that sharing her body with him would come easier, but…*c'est la vie*.

Ben let go a pent-up breath. "Look, April, is that what you came here for? To talk about our fathers? Because if it is, I can tell you that I don't—"

Impatient with herself, April squeezed her eyes shut, shook her head. "It's not. I—"

He blinked, seemingly surprised. "It's not?"

"No," she said.

He bit the corner of his lip, looking curiously relieved. "Then why did you come? Why are you here?"

Here it was, she thought. Truth or consequences time. She'd never been one to mince words, yet summoning the wherewithal to have this conversation with Ben was proving exceedingly difficult. She'd known it would be, but… Aw, hell. The fact was, she wasn't accustomed to *asking* men to sleep with her. Ordinarily, it was the other way around. They came to her. Furthermore, if she wanted someone, she'd never had to *tell* them. A loaded glance, a secret smile, an innocent yet promising touch.

Body language. Not the English language.

She hesitated, looked up and saw him waiting expectantly. Her heart began to pound. She couldn't believe she was going to do this, that she was actually going to *ask* him to have sex with her.

But she was.

Desperation had prodded other women to do worse, she told herself. And she was desperate.

Eighteen months.

Eighteen miserable, horribly unsatisfied months of unrelenting sexual agony. Frankie was right. If Ben couldn't pull an orgasm from her apparently comatose libido, then nobody could. She'd simply have to resign herself to a lifetime of sexual dysfunction. The idea was so abhorrent she had to smother a maniacal laugh. Hell, she'd probably go crazy. Turn into a cat-loving, batty old shrew who screamed at little children and collected empty butter tubs and bottle caps. She glanced nervously at him again.

"April?" he prodded. Concern had replaced expectation, pricking her conscience. "Is something wrong?"

She smothered a snort. "You could say that," she said, determined to go through with this. She pulled in a bracing breath, then let it go with a do-or-die whoosh. "I've got a personal problem…and I think you can help."

"A personal problem," he repeated.

"Yes," she managed to whisper over the litany of *Oh,God!Oh,God!Oh,God!* screaming in her head.

He hesitated for a moment. "Er, what sort of personal problem?"

"An *intimate* sort of problem," she confided with evidently just enough misery for him to make the connection.

A fleeting flash of surprise registered before he masked it with a less-jolted expression. In a nanosecond, though, a predatory gleam flared in his golden gaze and she suddenly felt as if she'd been caught between the crosshairs—*his*. "Of a sexual nature then?"

"Yes." She licked her suddenly dry lips and cleared her throat. Tried to look calm though she felt as though her intestines were going through the spin cycle. "For the past year and a half, I've been unable to— That is to say, I haven't— I can't—"

"Come?"

April nodded again. He could have said "reach orgasm" or "climax"—the more clinical term, she supposed—but "come" would work. "That sums it up nicely, yes," she replied.

Ben leaned back in his seat and bit his bottom lip, presumably to keep from smiling, the wretch. There was absolutely nothing funny about her condition. He regarded her with droll, brooding humor, his eyes a compelling combination of smoky arousal and intrigue. April lifted her chin and resisted the pressing urge to squirm.

"And you think that I can help you?" he asked in an infuriatingly calm voice. "Is that why you're here?"

"It is."

"Because you think that I can make you—"

"I do," she interrupted before he could finish, then resisted the urge to grin. "Provided your skill is in keeping with your reputation, that is," she added wryly.

Ben chuckled. "My reputation?"

April poked her tongue in her cheek, felt her lips quiver with a smile. "That's right. By all accounts—and I've heard many—you're quite a lover. You've even got a nickname. Haven't you heard it?" she asked innocently.

Ben leaned forward, let his elbows rest on his desk and steepled his fingers together. "A nickname?"

"Yep." She paused, purposely torturing him. *"The Vagina Whisperer,"* she shared dramatically. "Supposedly, you can make even the most reluctant kitty purr."

Ben's eyes widened, then he cracked up. "You have got to be kidding me."

I wish I were, April thought. Hearing about Ben's particular abilities, his legendary sexual prowess over the years had been a source of pain for her. To this day the idea of him touching another woman made her belly flip in a nauseated roll.

April had never been the jealous type. She'd always been secure enough in her own ability to attract and keep the opposite sex that she'd honestly never let jealousy get to her. Naturally she'd felt a twinge of it now and again—she'd hardly be human, otherwise—but frankly, she'd never been invested enough in another relationship to warrant jealousy.

And yet the mere thought of Ben with some-one else made her heartsick and absolutely wretched.

An unhappy truth lurked in that realization, but April determinedly refused to look for it. She'd mine her feelings later. Right now she had more pressing needs to take care of. Like eliminating the *someone elses* from Ben's bed and planting herself there instead.

"I'm not kidding," April finally told him. "That's why I'm here. Given the situation, I need someone with your particular brand of expertise to, er…remedy the situation. In exchange, I'll build you a Web site."

She felt ridiculous saying it—bartering her body for Web services, of all things—but it made it feel like more of a business proposition than a personal favor. Twisted reasoning, she knew, but it was the best she could do. If he could fix her— if he could give her the joy of a toe-curling, back-clawing, tingling tornadic orgasm—she'd gladly exchange services for services. He was good at sex. She was good at Web design. Different areas of expertise, but she'd work with what she had. It was better than feeling beholden.

Ben studied her, then after a prolonged moment, scrawled something on a piece of paper and handed it to her. "Seven o'clock," he said.

She frowned, looked at the piece of paper he'd handed her and discovered an address. His address, she realized belatedly. She glanced up with what she expected was an embarrassingly hopeful gaze. "Is this a yes, then? You'll help me."

The corner of his sexy mouth quirked up into a sinfully promising smile, one that told her he planned to help her until her eyes rolled back in her head and she sang every note of the Hallelujah chorus. "Oh, yeah," he said. "It's *definitely* a yes."

2

BEN LACED HIS FINGERS behind his head, leaned back in his chair and let a huge sigh balloon from his lungs as April closed his office door.

Sweet mother of God.

That had to be one of the most bizarre encounters he'd ever experienced in his life. In fact, he was still having trouble believing it. There were so many intriguing elements to their strange conversation that he had a hard time deciding where to start.

Eighteen months without an orgasm? Ironically, her climax had left town about the same time he'd started showing up at the Blue Monkey, Ben noted absently. And *The Vagina Whisperer?* Another silent chuckle bubbled up his throat. Still stunned, he didn't know whether to be flattered or offended. Ah, hell. Who was he kidding? He was damned flattered. After all, that nickname and what it implied was evidently what had brought April Wilson to his doorstep.

Looking for a sexual cure, no less.

From him.

When he'd been systematically running through every available woman in Louisiana trying to get her out of his head?

Suffering from a severe case of shock, he passed a hand over his face and laughed again. Had anyone told him when he'd rolled out of bed this morning and made his usual trek to the office that April would show up and *ask* him—*ask him*—to have sex with her, he would have never believed it. Instead, he would have told them to ditch the hallucinogenic drugs and seek professional help. Things like this just didn't happen to him. He'd always had to make his own luck.

Given the thin-lipped expression she'd adopted when the irony had all but gotten the better of him and he'd nearly laughed, Ben knew that his initial response—apart from shock—had annoyed the hell out of her. Not that he could blame her really. It couldn't have been easy to make the decision to seek his help, and frankly, he admired her for being both mature and blunt. That, in and of itself, was wholly refreshing. No games, no guesswork.

She could have just as easily made a play for him—which, given his recent behavior at the Blue Monkey, she knew he'd accept—and kept her motives to herself.

But she hadn't.

Instead, in a ballsy no-bullshit move, she'd leveled with him and suggested a mutually beneficial deal. And a deal was good—it leveled the playing field and encouraged emotional boundaries. Furthermore, he'd put off the effort and minutia involved with pulling together the necessary content for a proper Web page because, in truth, he hadn't found anyone whose work he admired as much as he did April's.

Her page was the perfect combination of professionalism and whimsy, gave the visitors and prospective clients an organized, aesthetic glimpse into who she was and what she could accomplish. She was damned good at what she did, Ben thought. She had an uncanny ability to interpret a theme and make that come together in a graphics format for her clients. She, too, was an artist. She merely worked in a different medium.

Ben paused considering. If April hadn't had an orgasm in eighteen months—*eighteen mind-boggling months*—then there had to be one helluva reason. Something more than just a string of sub-par lovers. Hell, even a premature ejaculator knew how to work his fingers. A grin tugged the edge of his mouth.

Or at the very least, she did.

He couldn't see her spending eighteen months in the equivalent of sexual purgatory without trying to tend to her own needs. Ben felt a smile tug at his lips. Not little Miss I-can-do-it-myself, he thought. That would be completely out of character. Her mother might have been a bona fide—quite frankly *disturbed*—bitch, but April could thank her for that my-way-or-the-highway attitude, if nothing else.

Thwarting her control freak of a mother had made April one of the most self-sufficient, stubborn and determined women he'd ever known. That trait, coupled with her inherent goodness—and the goodness she could detect in even the most undeserving people—her wicked sense of humor, a sure sense of herself and an innate sexuality that oozed from every pore, made her one of the most interesting, compelling women he'd ever been around.

Simply put, she charmed him. She always had. And knowing her the way he did, he was damned certain that she'd only considered asking for his help as a last-ditch effort to put an arc back into her evidently flatlined libido. He'd be willing to bet his left nut that she'd tried everything else, and when those options had failed, she'd decided to come to him.

Call him an opportunistic bastard, but he was glad.

And where others had failed, Ben thought with a slow smile, *he* would not.

The Vagina Whisperer rumor notwithstanding, he knew how to please a woman. As with anything, the desire to perform combined with the old "practice makes perfect" adage could turn even the most mediocre man or woman into a competent partner, but in Ben's opinion good lovers were born, not made.

Being a good lover involved more than knowing how to find a G-spot or administer the perfect kiss. A good lover had the inherent ability to seduce the mind, understood that planning a seduction went well beyond the traditional candles, wine and roses. Attention to detail, investing time, learning to listen, essentially picking up on her signals until a man knew her well enough to morph into *her* fantasy.

Most men had a tendency to rush the attraction, to hit the high spots for a mediocre payoff, when maybe just a few more days of patient consideration—priming, if you will—could result in a coupling so combustible the sheets all but set fire.

That was the kind of sex he specialized in.

He didn't waste his time with "dumbed down" sex. When he did it, he did it right. Clearly, April had been getting the dumbed-down variety for so long that her poor, confused libido had finally said "screw it" and gone into voluntary hibernation. That, or it had merely rebelled, waiting for the right guy to come along. Whatever the reason, she needed him, and simply knowing that made several organs swell, both north and south of his zipper.

Without warning, her plump, pouty mouth materialized too readily in his mind's eye and he felt a flame of heat lick his groin. God, he couldn't wait to kiss her again. Couldn't wait to push his tongue into the warm cavern of her mouth, taste the addictive combination of hot spice and sweet innocence and something else, something far more wonderful and bittersweet than either of the previously mentioned two—the flavor of being wanted.

Truly wanted.

Ben was accustomed to being desired, to being the object of a woman's lust. A come-hither smile, a bed-me look. Frankly, he got them all the time. He'd been blessed with decent good looks and a hefty dose of sex appeal. He couldn't deny it and wasn't above capitalizing on it when the urge struck. Which was often. He was a man, after all, and there was nothing politically correct about baser needs, the drive to procreate. He liked sex and didn't intend to apologize for it. But there was a huge difference between being *desired* and being *wanted*.

Desired—which was admittedly nice—was commonplace. But wanted was rare.

Wanted implied a familiarity, a longing despite flaws and imperfections. Wanted meant I'll take you warts and all. Ben swallowed. Wanted was just a hair shy of love, and the only time he'd ever felt that sort of connection—that sort of unconditional yearning—was with April.

She'd *wanted* him.

To know that she merely desired him now was a bit depressing, but when it came to her, he'd settle for whatever he could get. A bark of dry laughter erupted from his throat.

He'd willingly—gladly—be her whore.

Guess that didn't make him much different from his father after all, Ben thought as his lips twisted with bitter humor at the unwelcome insight.

Speaking of which, that raised another question. Did she know that her dad and his had become roommates? He'd wrongly assumed that had been the reason for her visit, and yet other than one awkward moment when she'd asked about his father, nothing else had been said about them. He'd sensed some tension, but if she'd known about their respective sires making the move to cohabit, she would have said something. Odd, then, that she hadn't.

He stilled. Surely to God she knew Marcus was gay, Ben thought, struck by the notion. He paused, mulling it over. Yeah, he scoffed. She *had* to know. How could she *not* know? Her parents had divorced years ago. He snorted. But considering who Marcus was married to, that argument wouldn't necessarily hold water.

April's unfortunate father could have cited any number of reasons for his belated departure from Morgana's evil side. Honestly, he didn't think he'd ever known another woman he disliked more. She was a cold, heartless, manipulative harpy and—

His mental tirade abruptly stopped and a slow dawning smile slid across his face.

—and she'd undoubtedly shit when she found out about April, Ben realized, unable to suppress the burst of vindictive glee that expanded in his chest.

And she'd definitely find out. Unless things had changed vastly over the years—and he highly suspected that they hadn't—April had never been able to make a move that her mother hadn't known about first. Ben chuckled again, rocked back in his chair once more and savored the idea of her chilly, furious face. Petty? Yes. But after the hell that selfish, vengeful bitch put him through, he didn't care.

What was it she'd said again when she'd warned him away? Oh, yeah. *"I've already lost a husband to your cracked-up white-trash father. I'll be damned before I'll lose my daughter to his filthy son."*

A regular little ray of sunshine she'd been, Ben thought, his insides churning with old unabsorbed hatred. Let her try to warn him away this time, dammit. He was ready for her.

"I DID IT."

Frankie whooped excitedly, forcing April to

momentarily pull the cell away from her ear. "Oh, thank God!" she said. "I'm so proud of you. One giant step for you, one small step for womankind. Way to buck that double standard, babe."

April smiled and carefully negotiated traffic. Ah, yes, the sexual double standard. Frankie's *biggest* pet peeve—though she had many—which made her a fantastic advocate for Chicks In Charge and a huge success as the movement's Carnal Contessa. Anything that smacked of a double standard or sexual repression made Frankie's blood boil. Of her three best friends, Frankie had been the most concerned over April's inability to reach climax.

"So how did it go? Did he *whisper* to you in his office?" she murmured with a wicked, suggestive purr. "Are you cured?"

April chuckled. "No and no. I'm supposed to meet him at his house at seven." Goose bumps erupted on her skin at the mere thought. To think that after all this time she was only hours away from a guaranteed orgasm. It almost made her light-headed.

"Oooh. So he's taking you to his lair, his den of iniquity, allowing you into the inter sanctum. Very, very interesting," she said, doing a comical

Einstein impression. "I figured a house call would be more in keeping with his style."

April would have, too, come to think of it. She couldn't be certain of course, but from everything she'd heard, Ben customarily guarded his personal space. He'd happily share another woman's bed, but if one had managed to actually share *his,* April had never caught wind of it.

"Or *multiple* house calls," Frankie continued. A wicked laugh bubbled up her throat. "What do you wanna bet that he prescribes more than one treatment?"

Would that she would be so lucky, April thought. After a year and a half with no conclusive action, she was due for more than one *treatment,* thank you very much.

"So tell me everything," her friend finally demanded. "What was he wearing?"

April laughed. "What does that have to do with anything?"

"You'll see," she said. "Indulge me."

"Er… Okay. Let's see." April paused, easily pulling Ben's image to the forefront of her mind. He was never very far away anyway. "He was wearing a dark almond handwoven wool sweater and a pair of khaki slacks." Both of which had looked fantastic on him. Very European. Very hot. The sweater had draped over those broad shoulders and muscled pecs, competently displaying the beautiful manly shape underneath.

"Any jewelry?"

"Aside from a designer watch—a TAG Heuer, I think—none that I could see."

"Looking that closely at him, eh?" Frankie said knowingly.

Aha, April thought, letting go a quiet laugh. She had been looking closely, evidently even more closely than she'd realized. But then again, Ben was hard *not* to look at.

Aside from being remarkably handsome—flawless bone structure, angular jaw, hollow cheeks, heavy-lidded soulful eyes and a slightly imperfect nose to add character—Ben had that whole mysterious *dark* thing going on. He could have easily stepped onto any gothic movie set and played the part of a sexy vampire or elusive shape-shifter…and she could just as easily see herself playing the role of his devoted familiar. He was…magnetic, April decided. God knows she'd always been drawn to him. Ben had that "It" quality, that certain charisma that put him leagues above the average guy.

"Well, now that Operation Orgasm is underway, would you like me to tell you about some good news I heard this morning?" Frankie asked.

Operation Orgasm? She'd named it? Sheesh. April shook her head. "Sure. What's up?"

"Carrie got a call from the producers of *Let's Cook, New Orleans!* this morning."

April squealed as a bolt of glee shot through her. "Oh, you're kidding!"

"I'm not," Frankie assured her, laughing herself. "She's meeting them next week. And she's a nervous wreck."

April guessed so. It wasn't every day that a person interviewed for their own television show. But with Carrie's looks—she had the face of an angel, the soul of a saint—which had been a plus considering she'd had to have the patience of one to work for that nitpicking bastard Martin, April thought—and a body that put every man who looked at her in the mood for sin. Between her good looks and incredible talent, the network would be foolish not to hire her.

Furthermore, Carrie needed the break. Chicks In Charge had given her an outlet of sorts, but the perpetual grind of working at a thankless job was beginning to wear on her. She'd worked hard for this, dammit. She deserved it.

"God, I hope this works out for her," April told her.

Frankie sighed. "Yeah. Me, too. I've got a call coming in," she said. "Keep me posted. I want details—the hot, the heaving and the horny. Call me as soon as you get home. Provided you come home," she added.

"Duly noted." With a soft chuckle, April disconnected, then made her way back to her home office. That was one of the benefits of her line of work.

Aside from the necessary legwork she liked to put into a project, ninety percent of her job was accomplished in the small gatehouse located at the rear of her property. She'd fallen in love with the main house, a stately Victorian in the Garden District, the instant she'd seen it. Between the money she'd managed to save and the trust fund she'd inherited at twenty-one, April had managed to pay cash in order to avoid a mortgage.

Her father's accountant had counseled against the move, had cited numerous investments she could have made in order to make the most of her money, but buying the house—owning her own place without fear of ever losing it—had been too important to her. If she never heard, "So long as you're living in my house…" or "My house, my rules," again, she'd die a happy woman. Frankly, she'd always hated living with her mother and from the time she was a little girl, she'd wanted her own place. Something that was solely hers.

Thankfully, in recent years her business had done well and thanks to the popularity of Chicks In Charge, she currently had more work that she could handle alone. She'd hired a couple of capable women from her local CHiC chapter to help out part-time. Aside from her estranged relationship with her father and the lengthy absence of an orgasm, her life was going remarkably well.

She was doing all she could do in regards to her father. When he was ready to share this new chapter of his life with her, he would. Did it hurt? Hell yeah. But apart from trying to maintain a presence in his life, what could she do?

Frankie had suggested hiring a private detective. For a few hundred dollars she could identify the significant someone in her father's life, but April couldn't bring herself to do it. It smacked too much of what her mother would do, and April purposely avoided any reason for comparison.

Undoubtedly her mother knew who her father was seeing—precious little escaped her ever-observant eye and if it did, her private detective kept her abreast of goings-on—but something about her mother's smug smile when the subject came up indicated to April that, for whatever reason, Morgana would take entirely too much glee in sharing her father's secret. And evidently, the only thing she'd enjoy more was her dad telling her himself.

But clearly her father didn't want her to know, and finding out by any other means seemed entirely too sneaky. She preferred the direct approach.

A smile tugged at the corner of her mouth. As evidenced by this morning's behavior. *Hi, Ben. My orgasm is broken and I need you to fix it for me.* Not verbatim, of course, but the meaning couldn't have been any more clear. Odd how their familiarity had both terrified and liberated her. Ben knew her, which had been both a pro and a con.

On the pro side, he knew what to expect from her. He knew that she didn't pull any punches, that she abhorred all methods of manipulation. That had given her the freedom to walk into his office and lay everything out on the line.

Then again, he *knew* her. It was like having your gyno and your ex being one in the same.

Talk about awkward. Hell, all that had been missing this morning was the paper dress and pair of stirrups.

At any rate, given the woeful twinge in her sex and the pleasant tingling sensation in her nipples, seeing *The Vagina Whisperer* had definitely been the right choice. She hadn't felt that much tension in her hot spots in over a year…and he hadn't even touched her yet.

April pulled into her driveway, shifted into park, then let her gaze turn inward. All he'd done was sit there and stare at her with those brooding, rock-your-world eyes. He'd calmly assessed her, trailed that compelling gaze over her body like warm honey over a biscuit and something inside her had wriggled to life once more. She was starving and, though it might be unreasonable, she knew beyond a shadow of a doubt that Ben was the only person who could feed her. April released a stuttering breath.

And the feast was at seven.

3

AT PRECISELY SEVEN O'CLOCK—she'd circled the block three times first in order to avoid being early—April pulled into Ben's driveway and tried to summon the courage to get out of her car. It was bad enough having to ask for an orgasm, but she had absolutely no intention of appearing too eager by preempting their prescribed meeting time. He knew she was desperate—she'd come to him, hadn't she?—but there was no need to look downright pathetic.

Though she'd gotten a good look at the classic Georgian on her numerous trips around the block, April leaned back in her seat and took a minute to really appreciate the old manor.

Painted a pale dove-gray and accented with crisp white shutters and trim, the house sat on an expertly manicured lawn surrounded by hundred-year-old live oaks dripping with Spanish moss that swayed in the chilly evening breeze. Ivy wound its way around the central columns supporting the huge porch and created an evergreen arbor, one she suspected would be dressed in lazy purple wisteria blossoms come the spring.

An ornamental iron fence surrounded the property and accompanying accent pieces had been strategically placed around the yard. Vintage gas lamps showcased twin dancing flames on either side of the curiously forbidding door.

Despite the obvious majesty of the home, there was a slightly gothic feel—one she imagined Ben purposely cultivated. It conjured images of mint juleps and voodoo dolls, and would have been right at home in an Anne Rice novel. She paused, absorbing the sensual essence of the house and decided it suited its owner. It was beautiful yet dark and seductive…full of hidden secrets.

April let out an expectant breath. But she wasn't here to explore hidden secrets. She was more interested in his hidden talents, ones she'd been fantasizing about for years and more recently, *today*.

Since this morning's conversation, every waking second had been consumed with the idea that Ben Hayes—the one guy that she'd always wanted—was going to make love to her.

Tonight.

For whatever reason, be it women's intuition or just wishful thinking, she was absolutely certain that he was going to be able to "fix" her, that whatever had prompted her orgasmic hiatus would crumble under the expert skill of his lovemaking.

A hot thrilling kiss from that sexy mouth, the slide of those big warm hands over her bare back, his talented tongue curling around her nipple. That big hard body positioned between her legs, pushing into her until he coaxed that elusive climax out of her dormant libido.

A sigh stuttered out of her lungs. All of it, hers for the taking the instant she drummed up the nerve to get out of the freaking car, she thought, annoyed with herself for dawdling. Asking for his help had been the hurdle, dammit. Walking through that door when she knew what awaited her should be a piece of cake.

And yet, she hesitated.

April didn't know why, couldn't pinpoint an exact cause for her anxiety, but for reasons she couldn't begin to explain, she knew—*knew*—that she was taking a huge risk. Knew that things couldn't as be as simple as what she hoped they'd be. No matter how she tried to simplify things, she'd invited Ben Hayes back into her life in one of the most intimate ways a woman could—into her body. There was nothing casual or commonplace about it and she didn't take it lightly.

In her opinion, there was nothing casual about sex. She'd had several lovers over the years, but they'd been chosen carefully. She had too much self-respect to hand her body over to someone who wouldn't appreciate it or be worthy of the gift. Despite their rocky past, if she hadn't known beyond a shadow of a doubt that Ben would fit the bill on both counts, she could have never gone to him and asked for his help.

Somewhere beneath that brooding exterior lay the sexy bad boy with the irreverent smile and kind heart she used to know. Finding him after all these years would be a chore, but she didn't doubt that he was still there. A faint smile curled her lips. She'd seen the briefest glimpse of him this morning.

With one last bracing breath, April snagged her purse and keys and got out of the car. It was do-or-die time, she thought, and, since she wasn't trying to sell him a vacuum cleaner or invite him to church, this was no front-door visit. Rather than taking the front walk, April followed the winding brick path alongside the house around to the back door. Another woeful twinge in her neglected sex prompted her to knock on the door.

Thirty seconds later, Ben appeared. Dressed in head-to-toe black, his dark hair still slightly damp and slicked away from his forehead, he looked sexy and dangerous, and completely capable of rocking her world. He smiled, just the merest quirk of his lips, and her toes curled.

"Come in."

If he'd take her in the mudroom, she could *come* now, April thought, wondering if this was what it felt like to be held enthralled. One look and those two little words and she was utterly enchanted. Captivated. As a teenager he'd been addictive—as an adult, he was positively lethal.

This was the problem, a little-heeded voice said. *You'll care too much and he'll break your heart again. And this time, you won't get over it.*

"Hi," April said, too breathlessly, in her opinion, and determinedly ignored the sound voice of reason. "I hope I'm not early."

"Right on time," he told her, eyes twinkling with perceptive humor. Undoubtedly he'd seen her driving around the block, she thought, mortified. Before she could dwell on it, though, he calmly laced his fingers through hers, causing a tingle to race up her arm, and tugged her gently toward the parlor. He released her hand and made his way to an ornate bar stationed in the corner of the room. "Can I get you something to drink?"

April nodded, glanced idly around the room, pretending to look at anything but him. "Sure. A beer would be nice."

He shot her a look over his shoulder. "Abita golden, right?"

Surprised that he'd paid that close attention to her beverage of choice—and that he'd obviously gone to the trouble to get it—April's anxiety lessened considerably.

A cozy fire burned in the grate, the intimate flames casting eerie shadows on the hand-painted, most likely imported, wallpaper. Genuine antiques and excellent reproductions anchored the room, and a beautiful Oriental rug lay over the dark-stained hardwood floors. Whoever had decorated for him—and who knows, April thought, he could have done it himself—had done an excellent job marrying masculine colors to heavy furnishings with distinctive feminine curves. No hard lines. Just lots of rounded edges and scrollwork. Very evocative. Very sensual.

Very Ben.

No decorator, April decided. There'd been too much attention to detail for anyone else to have captured his particular style.

He ambled over and she accepted her beer. "You have a lovely home."

"Thanks," he told her. "Getting it right has been a process, but it's coming along."

She smiled. Ah. So she'd been right. "How long have you lived here?"

"Six years." He sipped his wine, unwittingly wetting his lips. "What about you? You're still in the Garden District, too, right?"

"I am," she said cautiously. He'd kept up with her that well, had he? Her internal temperature jumped another degree as a pleasant warmth moved into her belly.

Ben easily settled himself onto a serpentine sofa, took another drink of his wine and regarded her over the rim. "I've been thinking about your problem," he said.

A shiver arced up her spine. "You have?"

"Yes." He paused. "If it's all the same to you, I'd like to have a little more information."

Though she could have sat in any number of places in the room, April chose the spot next to him on the other end of the sofa. His plan, she knew. He'd purposely sat first, forcing her to make the choice to come to him. Testing her? she wondered. Or reinforcing the idea? "Er...what kind of information?"

Quite frankly, she never dreamed that he'd think past sleeping with her. She couldn't decide whether to be flattered or offended. Ultimately, she decided to reserve judgment until she knew precisely what sort of information he was interested in.

"The personal sort. Tell me again when your problem started?"

She supposed that was a fair question. "About eighteen months ago."

"Any mitigating circumstances?"

April quirked a questioning brow. "Mitigating circumstances?"

Ben cleared his throat. "A bad experience."

What was he talking about? "Bad sex?"

"Rough sex," he corrected. "That sort of thing."

April's eyes widened. "No, no. Nothing like that." Though, quite honestly, it damned sure hadn't been anything to write home about. Her last relationship had ended when her boyfriend of more than a year had dumped her when she'd suddenly lost the ability to climax. His ego had been too fragile, she supposed, though she had to admit, if the situation had been reversed, she would have been a wee bit intimidated, as well.

Nevertheless, she damned well wouldn't have quit trying after a measly two-week dry spell. A real fighter he'd turned out to be, April thought with a mental eye roll. Better to find out now rather than later, she supposed. Still…

"Good," Ben replied, seemingly relieved. He turned to look at her. "So what you're saying is that, for no obvious reason, you suddenly couldn't—"

"That's right."

He frowned, apparently puzzling over her unique problem. "Were you in a relationship at the time?"

"Several," she deadpanned, just to rattle him.

His startled gaze swung to hers.

"With Mike, my mechanic," she confided. "Man, the things he could do with a socket wrench and a can of WD-40," she lamented with a dramatic sigh, thoroughly enjoying the slight choking noise Ben made. She resisted the urge to smile. "He hung around until he realized that no amount of elbow grease was going to get the job done."

She paused, seemingly trying to remember her vast cache of lovers. "Then there was Allen, my UPS guy. *Mmm.Mmm.Mmm. What can brown do for you?*" She manufactured another woebegone sigh. "The instant my delivery confirmation went AWOL, it was over between us." April cocked her head. "Only Beth had the balls to hang around— figuratively speaking, of course," she added, throwing in a lesbian relationship just for the hell of it. "She works for the Audubon Zoo, but even she couldn't get past the misery of continually failing to give me release when my Big O went the way of the buffalo." She smiled and bit her lip. "I'm banking on you having a bit more fortitude."

Ben's lips slid into a grin and those compelling amber eyes twinkled with humor. "The way of the buffalo, eh?"

"Or the dodo. Whatever analogy works best for you." She grinned. "I *was* in a relationship when it happened," she finally told him. "I'd been in one for more than a year, as a matter of fact."

His gaze sharpened. "So it was serious then?"

April thought about it. "It was getting there, I suppose. We'd considered moving in together." Actually, come to think of it, her orgasm had vanished shortly after they'd started making tentative plans for him to move in with her. Could that have had something to do with it? April wondered now, considering the connection.

Ben studied her. "Could have been your body's way of telling you that you were with the wrong guy."

"Could be," she conceded. "But that doesn't explain why I haven't been able to take care of business myself." April stilled. Did she really just tell Ben Hayes about her failed masturbation attempts? she wondered, blushing to the roots of her hair. Granted, it was something she didn't mind discussing with other women, but it was the first time she'd ever made a confession of that nature to a guy, for heaven's sake. Especially a hot one, whom she couldn't wait to get into bed.

Geez. Would her humiliation never end?

A slow grin rolled across Ben's lips and, for whatever reason, she got the distinct impression that he was imagining her stretched out naked on cool sheets, *taking care of business*. His lids dropped to half-mast and those amber orbs darkened a shade. "No," he murmured softly. "It doesn't, does it?" He paused. "I am certain that I have the *fortitude*—" he lingered suggestively over the words "—to take care of you, but I'm going to ask that you have patience."

Oh, hell. That didn't sound good. She'd run out of patience, dammit. That's why she'd finally come to him. "Patience?"

Ben's compelling gaze tangled with hers and held. "I think that your problem is more in your head than in your sex."

April felt her hackles rise. "You think I need to see a shrink?"

"No," he said smoothly. "If I can't make you come, then I think you need to see a doctor."

It's not as if she hadn't heard that before, April thought. Frankie had given her the same sort of advice. Still, she didn't get it. Had he changed his mind? Did he, God forbid, *not* want to have sex with her? Had those smoldering looks been a figment of her imagination? Had she been that far off base assuming that he wanted her, too? Oh, God. Her stomach rolled and every ounce of moisture evaporated from her mouth.

She abruptly stood, looked for a coaster to leave her beer on and, not finding one, decided to take it with her. "You know, I'm not altogether sure this was such a good idea after all. I—"

Ben set his drink aside and calmly found his feet. He chuckled softly, the sound intimate like the rustle of sheets. "Oh, it's definitely a good idea."

"But—"

He stalked toward her. "It's not that I don't want you, April," he said, correctly—disturbingly—guessing her fears. "You know I do. That's why you came to me." His hands framed her face and he angled her mouth up toward his. "Here," he murmured huskily, skimming his thumb over her bottom lip. "Let me prove it."

Slowly, reverently, as though he had all the time in the world, Ben searched her face—really looked at her—then lowered his lips until they touched hers, sparking a reaction in her body that for all intents and purposes made New Orleans's famed Mardi Gras celebration look like a pathetic little party with a single sparkler and a broken piñata.

Fireworks detonated in her belly, pushing bright-colored flames of happiness and longing coursing through her blood until her knees buckled and she sagged against him. Beer still in hand, April wound her arms around his neck and aligned herself against him, savoring the feel of Ben's mouth ravaging hers. Sucking, stroking…dark, seductive…and woefully familiar. He might have improved on the technique, but the flavor was still the same.

Positively sinful.

A lick of heat enflamed her sex and for the first time in over a year and a half, she felt the initial quickening of genuine arousal deep in her womb. With a mewl of pleasure, she smiled against his lips, pushed her free hand into the hair at his nape and excitedly deepened the kiss.

She'd been right. He could fix her. And the power to heal lay just behind his zipper.

Or in his fingers.

Or in his mouth.

And hell, for all she knew, in his feet.

Whatever it was, he had it in spades and she wanted him more than she'd ever wanted anyone. Could feel his fingers trembling against her face, his heart pounding wildly against her chest. Something about that quaking touch made her eyes involuntarily mist.

Oh, Ben, she thought.

Much to her dismay, he reluctantly ended the kiss. "I want you," he murmured, his voice a throaty purr. "Do you believe me now?"

Unable to speak, April nodded.

"Then I want you to trust me." He nuzzled her neck. "You don't need sex, April—you need a seduction."

A broken chuckle erupted from her throat. Oh, but she begged to differ. She drew back, ready to argue, but he kissed her again silencing her protest.

"You just need someone to work for it—to work for *you*," he continued. "You need someone who'll walk across the street to feel the chill of your shadow. Someone who will show up at a pub every Friday night for the past year and a half just to breathe the same air. You need someone who will eat, breathe and live making you happy, making you *want*. By the time I truly bed you, you're going to want me so desperately that you'll come for me before I take you. Then I'll take you and you'll come again."

She shuddered, shaken by the scenario he'd painted. "But I do want you."

"No, you *desire* me. There's a difference."

"Semantics."

He suckled her bottom lip once more. "Trust me," he whispered.

And curiously, she did.

4

BEN SLOWLY RELEASED HER when every instinct he possessed screamed for him to hold on to her and never let her go. To strip her naked, then stretch her ripe body out on the rug beneath their feet and pump into her until every last bit of energy he possessed was gone, given to her.

And he would…but not right now. She wasn't the only one who was going to have to be patient. He'd waited this long, dammit. A few more days—a week at the most—wouldn't kill him. He smothered a laugh. It might drive him crazy, but death was hardly imminent.

In the meantime, there were some ground rules he felt they needed to cover. Ben slid a hand down her arm, laced his fingers through hers then tugged her back toward the couch.

"Before this goes any further, I want to lay out a few ground rules. Do you have any objections?"

Her plump bottom lip still swollen from his kiss, April shot him a look. "Depends on the rules," she said warily, her clear green eyes suddenly guarded.

He tried not to laugh. "Okay. Rule Number One. For the next week, when I call, you come to me. No arguments, no buts, no excuses. I call, you come."

High-handed? Yes. But necessary. For the next week, Ben was going to become her dream lover. Every move he made would be orchestrated for her pleasure, her enjoyment, her excitement and there was nothing more exciting than the courage to surrender and the thrill of the unknown.

When he called, she'd have to let go and then wonder what he had planned. Initially she'd resist, but in the end he knew she'd come to enjoy it…then wait for it. As with any reward, expectation was half the fun. He made a mental note to get her e-mail address, IM screen name and cell number.

Predictably, April didn't look happy. She considered him thoughtfully, seemed to be weighing the ramifications which could arise out of a power-shifting deal. Finally, she nodded. "Okay. I'll do that for you…provided you do that for me. *I* call, *you* come."

Ben chuckled. He should have expected this. What the hell, he decided. This was her fantasy, after all. "Fine," he agreed. "Now...Rule Number Two. Beyond tonight, no talking about our parents. Not your father, not my father, not your mother." He couldn't help the edge that entered his voice when he mentioned Morgana. "The past is the past and I want to leave it there." *Vast understatement,* he thought. "Understood?"

A perplexing line emerged between her brows and something in that clear green gaze sharpened and probed, attempting, he imagined, to penetrate his thoughts.

She bit her lip, shoved a handful of curly hair behind her ear. "Okay," she said at last and Ben let go of a breath he hadn't been aware he'd been holding. "But I want to clear the air about something first."

Ben braced himself. This was a conversation long overdue—he owed it to her, he knew—but that didn't keep him from dreading it with every fiber in his being. Frankly, having buzzards feast on his privates held greater appeal. Reluctantly, he nodded, silently giving her the go-ahead.

"My mother might have issued a you-can-look-but-don't-touch order, but *I* didn't." A sad smile shaped her lips. "Did you respect her that much, or was I just not worth it?"

Ben swallowed. He knew he'd hurt her when they were younger, but until this very moment, he'd never realized exactly how much. An ache pricked his heart, and for the millionth time over the past ten years, he wished like hell that he had fought for her. That he'd told her mother to rot in hell and loved April the way he'd wanted to.

"Neither," he said, his voice curiously rusty. "Believe me, April, I feel a lot of things for your mother, but—" he chuckled darkly "—respect isn't one of them. As for you being worth it…" He looked up and caught her gaze. Difficult though it was, she deserved sincerity. Ben conjured a smile. "Babe, you were always worth it. Things just— Things just got complicated and I was young and stupid. Not much of an excuse, I know, but…" He shrugged, unable to tell her the whole truth. Repeating what her mother had told him only gave the bitch more power. He wouldn't do it, wouldn't give her the satisfaction. There were some people who were born simply to be the bane of mankind's existence and Morgana Wilson was one of those people. There was no rhyme, reason or motivation for her hateful behavior. It just *was*.

April chewed the corner of her lip, seemingly absorbing his thin excuse for breaking her heart. Finally, she nodded. "Well, I know you're older," she said matter-of-factly. "Are you smarter?"

Ben laughed, oddly relieved. "I'm a genius."

"Good," she said. "I was hoping a little wisdom had come with age." She paused. "She'll hear about us, you know." She rolled her eyes. "She hears about everything. I'm sure she has a guy on payroll just to keep her informed of my comings and goings. I, uh… I just want to make sure that you're up for the fallout this time."

He cocked his head and shrugged. "Let her bring it on," he said, leaning back against the sofa. "We're of age. It's not like she can threaten me with statutory rape this time."

April gasped. "What?"

Ben swore. He hadn't meant to say that. Truth be told, Morgana's threatening to charge him with statutory rape if he touched her daughter again hadn't had anything to do with why he'd avoided April. It was the other little poisoned bombshells she'd dropped on his world that had prevented him from continuing their relationship. Nevertheless, it was the truth—better than "things got complicated," at any rate. "I would have thought she'd told you."

April scowled and her delicate jaw hardened. "She never told me anything." She laughed bitterly. "No, I take that back. She'd told me that you were 'a horny boy looking to dip your wick and that I was a fool if I thought I was special to you. Good riddance,' she'd said."

God, what a hateful bitch, Ben thought, every muscle atrophying with anger. "Did you believe her?"

April shrugged. "When you never came back? What choice did I have?" She said it offhand, as if it didn't matter. But the melancholy look in her eyes said otherwise.

"I *was* horny," Ben admitted. "Show me any teenage boy—or any man—who says he's not and I'll show you a liar." He cleared his throat, lowered his voice. "But you *were* special, April." She still was and he'd prove it to her this week.

Again, that sad smile. "You broke my heart."

"And yet you asked for my help."

"I asked for sex, Ben. I didn't ask to pick up where we left off."

His senses went on alert. "Is that a warning?"

She shook her head, seemed to be measuring him. "Just a clarification."

"Are you opposed to it turning into more?" He

was, dammit. Or he should be. There were too many complications. What in the hell was he doing?

She hesitated. "I... I don't know. Ask me again at the end of the week. So," she said briskly, her crisp tone indicating a swift subject change. "Have you thought about what you'd like to see for your page?"

Back to business, to their deal. For whatever reason, the speedy departure from the personal to the jarring reminder of their agreement made Ben's stomach sour. Just this morning he'd thought the idea of exchanging services was a good idea, but after one kiss and an awkward but therapeutic clear-the-air conversation, he was ready to abandon the plan. This was not good, he decided, irritated with himself. Losing focus this early into their reunion didn't bode well.

"Er...yeah," he said, rubbing the back of his neck. Ben quickly outlined what he thought would work.

"That gives me somewhere to start," April said. "If you don't mind, e-mail me a few sites that you find appealing. I'm not interested in copying them, I just want to make sure that we're on the same page, so to speak. I'll need a full bio, as well as images of all the work you'd like featured on the site. If you wouldn't mind, categorize them. You know, early work, middle years, and most recent. Also list any pertinent awards you'd like me to add."

"I'll have my secretary forward everything to you in the morning."

"Excellent." April glanced at her watch. "Well…it's getting late. I, uh…I should go."

Ben didn't want her to leave, but he stood all the same. He accepted her beer, then set it aside and helped her from the sofa. Her small hand fit snugly in his, causing a warm tingling feeling to grow in his chest. Indigestion, he thought, knowing it was a lie.

"So what's next?" April asked.

Ben smiled, and followed her through the house. "I'll call you," he said, alluding to Rule Number One.

"Not if I call you first," April said, shooting a sly look over her shoulder. She paused by the back door. "I like this," she said. "Talking to you again."

Code for I've missed you, Ben decided, heartened by her sheepish admission. He sidled closer to her, let his gaze travel over the achingly familiar curves of her face. God, she was beautiful. "I've missed you, too."

Ben lowered his head, pressed his lips lightly to hers—an appetizer of what was to come—then summoned the strength to draw back. "Until…"

She blinked a little drunkenly. "Until when?"

He grinned. "I guess we'll see."

A soft chuckle bubbled up her throat and, gratifyingly, he saw the first spark of adventure light those gorgeous green eyes. "Until when, then," she said. And still smiling, she walked out into the night.

Too bad he couldn't follow her, Ben thought. Home… To the ends of the earth… He passed a weary hand over his face and leaned against the doorjamb. Hell, he wasn't picky.

Evidently just stupid. Because he didn't stand a chance in hell of not falling in love with her all over again.

"…YES, LEESA, I got your note. I'll get someone on those updates right away." April quickly forwarded her client's request to Margo, one of her assistants, then set to work on Ben's site. As he'd said, his secretary had promptly sent her all of the necessary information this morning, with a promise to "extort" captions for the photos as well as a welcome commentary for the home page from Ben as soon as possible.

Rather than working on other projects, April had come in this morning and pawned them off on her help. Since she was finding it impossible to think of anything other than Ben, she figured she might as well take advantage of her fixation and get to work on his design.

After poring over the information and photos that Claudette had sent her, and playing around with various backgrounds, April had eventually gone back to one photograph that had initially caught her eye.

It was a sepia-toned still-life print of a huge— at least two-hundred-year-old—gnarled live oak. Its massive trunk was knotty and weather- beaten, its branches just as twisted and worn. But there was something secure and al- most…reverent about the space beneath the tree's canopy. It was living history and live shel- ter, vulnerable, but strong. Dark, forbidding and peaceful.

A lot like Ben, she decided.

She was suddenly hit with an arousing thought—wouldn't it be incredible to make love with Ben beneath the sheltering branches? Something about the history, the permanence, the raw elemental power of nature and all it represented tugged at her.

After only the smallest bit of debate, she lightened the frame a couple of shades, then set it as the background. The various hues of brown and black achieved the dark, polished look she was aiming for. She'd inserted Ben's equally mysterious black-and-white head shot in the upper left-hand corner—geez, the man was beautiful—then added a ragged parchment-paper-looking toolbar with the corresponding links across the top. The effect reminded her of an old postcard.

So far, so good, she thought, pleased with the way it seemed to be coming together. She'd send the initial mock-up—as well as a few others just for good measure—to Ben and see what he thought, but she fully expected him to be drawn to this design. It wasn't conceit, just fact. She was usually pretty good at pegging what a client would like, what they would respond to. She could almost always—

April stilled as the little whistle that heralded an incoming Instant Message sounded in her quiet office. She saved her work, closed out of the program, then moved to her Internet window.

BenHayes: Hey, are you there?

April smiled, bit her lip and felt her heart begin to pound. Her belly gave an odd quiver.

AprilWilson: Yeah…I'm here.

BenHayes: Good, cause I want you here.

Her toes curled.

AprilWilson: Where is here? Am I supposed to be psychic? <g>

BenHayes: Change into something pretty and meet me at the riverfront, pier eighteen in an hour.

Pier eighteen? she wondered. What was at pier eighteen?

AprilWilson: How do you know I'm not already wearing something pretty?

BenHayes: LOL, let me rephrase that—change into something *sexy* and meet me in an hour.

Ridiculously excited, April bit the inside of her cheek.

AprilWilson: Gotcha. Any hints?

BenHayes: Sorry, no. Just be there.

AprilWilson: I will….

Still wearing a goofy smile, April watched Ben log off, then kicked back in her chair and let her imagination run wild. Pier eighteen? She'd been thinking about this seduction he had planned—hell, how could she not?—and had expected him to take her to dinner first. Someplace quiet and expensive. Romantic. That's usually what came to mind when one typically thought of romance.

But the last thing she expected was a trip to the waterfront in something sexy. She should have known better. There had never been anything typical about Ben Hayes.

Oh, hell, April thought as she bolted upright. She didn't have time to sit around and fantasize about what he had planned for her—she had to get ready. She snagged her purse, bid a quick farewell to Margo and Joyce, then made the brisk walk up front to her house.

If she hurried, she'd have time to run a razor over her legs and work some magic with her hair.

As for the something sexy, she'd pull out her trusty little black dress and class it up with a pair of Emilio Pucci slingbacks. It wasn't often that she'd splurge on something so expensive, but she'd been unable to resist the bright colors and cool style. Besides, every woman needed one pair of power shoes and the Pucci slingbacks were hers.

Thirty minutes later she was in her car, headed toward the waterfront. She had to admit, when Ben had first mentioned Rule Number One, she'd been reluctant to play along. Being at someone's beck and call wasn't ordinarily her idea of fun. Odd then that she was finding it so thrilling now. The thrill of the unknown, the idea that she was playing hooky from work, doing something spontaneous and slightly wicked.

And to think she could do it to him, too, April thought with a giddy laugh. Having Ben at her beck and call…oh, my, the possibilities were endless. Come to think of it, he'd looked a little startled at her stipulation, but then he could hardly ask her to do something he wasn't willing to do himself, now could he? It wasn't sporting.

As for Rule Number Two…that one puzzled her. She didn't altogether understand why the subject of their parents was off-limits—aside from her mean-spirited psychotic mother, April thought, seething all over again. *That* she could completely understand. Statutory rape? Please, she would have been eighteen in a couple of months. It was just like her mother to threaten something so heinous.

Even though the warning had been a legitimate excuse, April couldn't help but think that there had to have been more to it. Ben had been curiously evasive last night, not necessarily reluctant, but not altogether forthcoming, either. Hell, she'd only learned about the statutory rape issue because he'd let it slip, and she couldn't help but wonder if there would be more he might unwittingly reveal over the next week.

Furthermore, why on earth would he consider their fathers off-limits? April knew that Ben and his father had had a slight falling-out shortly after their relationship had ended, but she'd always chalked it up to typical teenage behavior. Now she wasn't so sure. Something about Ben's demeanor didn't sit right. She couldn't exactly put her finger on it, but it sure as hell made her wonder all the same.

Besides, what could *her* father possibly have to do with anything? Her dad might have his faults, but he'd always been good to Ben's family, particularly his father. Unable to hold a steady job after Vietnam, her father had given Davy Hayes a permanent home for his family and a steady income. What could Ben possibly find wrong with that? A frown inched its way across her forehead. It just didn't make any sense. Then again, she could be reading more into Ben's motives than what was actually there.

At any rate, she would abide by his rules. Quite frankly, she wasn't interested in discussing their parents this week anyway. April harrumphed. Visions of her disapproving mother and distant father were hardly conducive to getting her orgasm back. So as far as she was concerned, the further they were away from her mind over the next seven days, the better.

As for her shaky history with Ben, she'd said her piece last night. She'd addressed the elephant in the room because she'd been certain that moving forward without letting the other go would have been difficult. Doable, but difficult. Just keeping things on a sexual level and her silly heart disengaged was going to be hard enough.

April knew that she'd never fully gotten over Ben. He'd always been her secret love, that special someone who couldn't be replaced. She'd moved on, had managed to have normal relationships with other men, but he'd always been there in the back of her mind, a ruler by which she measured every other guy.

He'd been special.

And this week with him would either solidify that youthful impression—prove that it wasn't just her imagination, that he had been the guy of her dreams—or dispel the fantasy once and for all.

Either outcome put her heart in danger.

What was it he'd said last night? *Are you opposed to it becoming more?* Meaning, would you like this to be more than sex? Though she'd given him a guarded, sophisticated answer last night, deep in the place where wishes grew, she did long for it to become more. She couldn't help it.

But she was no longer the doe-eyed teenager convinced that she'd die without him. She was a self-sufficient single woman who could take care of herself and she was proud of what she'd accomplished. Would she like a man in her life? Sure, so long as it was the *right man*.

While it was possible that Ben could be the one for her, it was equally possible that he wasn't. She'd seen too many women compromise their independence and good sense just for the sake of a ring on their finger. She'd bought her own damned ring, thank you very much, and it sparkled just as much—if not more—because of it.

No doubt she was worrying about it for nothing. Just because Ben had seemed curious about her feelings for him, for all she knew, he could have been merely feeling her out to avoid a sticky entanglement once she got her orgasm back. A patient rarely saw a doctor after the cure, right? Once things were back to normal, unless they were both interested in pursuing the relationship, there'd be no cause to continue. For whatever reason, she found the idea wholly depressing.

April found a parking place as close to pier eighteen as she could, then shifted into park and tried to shake off her heavy thoughts. She was borrowing trouble, dammit. For the next week all she wanted to think about was letting Ben *whisper* her back from the brink of sexual extinction. She wanted to exercise Rule Number One herself—put *him* at *her* beck and call—and finally, blessedly, have sex with the one guy in the world she'd always wanted to have in her bed.

God, how many times had she fantasized about this? About him? About what it would be like to feel that hard body buried deep within hers? That hot mouth feeding at her breasts, then between her legs?

Smooth warm skin, hard muscles, the slide of his talented hand over her thigh. Ben, naked and needy and hers.

April let out a shuddering breath as her nipples pearled beneath her dress. That woeful buzz pinged her sex once more, causing her belly to clench with awareness.

And why in the hell was she sitting out here fantasizing about Ben when the genuine article was waiting for her? Sheesh. Irritated, April vaulted from the car. Now that was hardly graceful. With her luck, he was probably watching her again. She needed professional help. She really did.

Muttering angrily under her breath, she followed the walk down to pier eighteen, then started to look for Ben.

She didn't have to look far…and her anger swiftly turned to astonishment.

Smiling—evidently he had witnessed her graceless exit from the car—Ben stood on the deck of a sailboat. He wore a pair of khaki slacks and a navy-blue cable-knit sweater. He held a couple of empty champagne glasses loosely in one hand. The afternoon breeze ruffled the ends of his dark hair, and though he was hardly dressed the part, she was strongly reminded of a pirate. A quick glance at the name of the boat—*Shutter-bug*—told her that it was his.

Astounded, April grinned up at him. "Permission to come aboard, Captain?"

He eyed her up and down, slowly, thoroughly, until she felt the tops of her thighs warm beneath that intense, slumberous scrutiny. Evidently her little black dress passed muster because she had the privilege of watching those light brown eyes darken into a smoky bedroom hue…a silent invitation to sin. "Permission granted," he said. "Come aboard."

Oy. Would that she could be so lucky.

5

BEN SET ASIDE the champagne flutes he'd been holding and offered April a hand up. The instant her palm connected with his, he felt an odd, warm tingling start in his fingers and, eventually, infect his whole body. No matter how many times he touched her—no matter how casual or innocent the contact—he still felt as if he'd been dunked in champagne. It was an altogether unnerving experience, one he equally craved and dreaded.

A smile curling her lush mouth, April climbed aboard and shot him a look that confirmed she'd enjoyed the mystery of Rule Number One as much as he'd thought she would. Those clear green eyes sparkled with excitement and anticipation, and realizing he took credit for them made his chest inflate with a ridiculous amount of pride.

Now would be a good time to say something smooth and romantic—something fantasy worthy—yet Ben found himself unable to do either. Instead, he simply stared at her.

She'd uh… She'd definitely taken the "sexy" order to heart, Ben thought, as a blast of heat detonated in his loins. Her long hair was pulled up into a knot of curls, exposing the vulnerable nape of her neck and showcasing the sweet curve of her jaw. With the exception of her lips, which were painted a shockingly sensual red, she'd kept her makeup to a minimum, allowing the healthy glow of her skin to shine through.

Then there was the dress. Ben covertly pulled in a gulp of much-needed air, then slowly exhaled through his nose. He could sum it up in three words.

Short. Tight. Black.

Wait, make that four—*hot*.

The stretchy fabric clung to her body and accentuated each and every curve. The lush mounds of her breasts, the small indentation of her waist and the gentle swell of her womanly hips. April was all woman, firm where she should be firm and soft where she should be soft. By Hollywood standards she'd be considered overweight, but there was absolutely nothing fat about her. Soft and lush, her form was reminiscent of a forties pinup model. His gaze traveled the length of her, stopping long enough to appreciate her toned legs, then rested at her feet.

His lips quirked. "Nice shoes."

She dimpled. "But hardly practical. I didn't know you sail."

"Practical is overrated," he said. "Especially when you look that hot."

She chewed the inside of her cheek and blushed adorably. "I don't know how hot I'm going to look when we're out on the water. I didn't bring a coat."

Ben chuckled softly, then looked out over the harbor. "Trust me, you're not going to need one."

She raised an exaggerated brow, then laughed. "So," she said, blowing out an expectant breath. "Where are we going?"

Ben calmly filled a flute and handed it to her. "Don't worry about it. You're just along for the ride."

She cocked her head. "Is that right?"

"It is." He gestured toward a seat for her, then began to loosen the moorings. "Have you ever seen New Orleans from the water at night? Ever watched her glow alive with neon and light?"

April shook her head. He could feel her gaze on him as he worked, peering intently, as though trying to absorb his secrets. He'd better be careful. If she looked too closely she'd discover that he was still head over heels in love with her. The admission wasn't an easy one, but after last night—that single soul-shattering kiss—he'd had to admit it. At least to himself, at any rate.

Ben glanced up at her. "Then you're in for a treat."

Twenty minutes later they were out in the harbor, cruising along at a steady clip. April's hair had quickly come loose from its up-do, causing curly stands to whip away from her face. She wore a perpetual smile, let the kiss of the evening chill blow over her face. Occasionally she'd take a sip of her champagne, but for the most part she looked content to simply enjoy the ride.

Ben found his favorite spot, then dropped anchor. He made a quick trip to the galley, then came back up with a wicker basket laden with a fruit and cheese spread. He settled in next to April—close enough to keep her warm, as he'd promised—and handed her a china plate.

"Blue Willow," she said, eyeing the dish appreciatively.

"It was my grandmother's. She believed in using the good stuff all the time."

April selected a few strawberries and a small bunch of grapes. "Wise woman, your grandmother. I firmly believe in using the good stuff, too."

Ben stacked a piece of cheese on top of an apple wedge, then shot her a smile. "As evidenced by your shoes."

"Hey," she said, her voice rife with mock indignation, "these are my only pair of Pucci shoes."

"And you wore them for me?"

"No," she replied with a haughty sniff. "I wore them for me. You said sexy." She lifted her foot and turned it this way and that, admiring the style. "And you've got to admit, these are sexy shoes." She put her foot down and resumed eating.

Ben felt a chuckle vibrate in the back of his throat. "They are. On you," he added softly.

Her lips twitched with the effort not to smile. "So when did you start sailing?" she asked. "Is the *Shutterbug* a recent acquisition or have you had her awhile?"

"I've had her awhile. A couple of years."

"So why the sudden interest?"

Ben took a sip of his drink, relaxed more fully against the seat…and purposely into her. "A client, actually. I was commissioned to take pictures of his waterfront home and he insisted the best shots could be achieved from the water. He was right, by the way," Ben added. "At any rate, he had a thirty-one-footer, much like this one, and I got the bug." He shrugged. "I loved it, being out on the water, harnessing the wind." He looked back toward the ever-changing shoreline and let go a small sigh. "It's peaceful, don't you think?"

Beside him he sensed April following his gaze. He felt her body deflate with a soft breath as she took in the various lights beginning to define the city's skyline. Within a matter of minutes, dusk would make way for darkness and the whole town would be glowing before them. Ben didn't speak, but waited for that moment. He slid an arm around her shoulders, tucking her more tightly against him, then absently doodled on her upper arm with his fingertip through the slinky fabric of her dress. The waves lapped at the hull, creating an intimate music around them.

Finally, darkness fell and the city shone like a kaleidoscopic jewel nestled against the riverbank. April's breath caught and she uttered a single "oh" of delighted pleasure.

Ben's own breath stalled as her joy mushroomed inside him. Being here with her, feeling the gentle rise and fall of her shoulder next to him, the warmth of her body—her very essence—had to be one of the most perfect things he'd ever experienced. It had been so long since he'd enjoyed anything close to genuine happiness, it took him several seconds to make the connection.

He leaned in and nuzzled her neck, absorbing her scent, something sweet and musky and only hers. Gratifyingly, she shivered, and inclined her head to give him better access.

Aha. He had her, Ben thought. Time to put her proper seduction into motion. The sooner she was primed, the sooner he'd be able to ease the ache in his loins, and more importantly, hers. That's what this was about, he reminded himself.

Her.

And he knew beyond a shadow of a doubt she'd be more than worth it.

APRIL'S EYES DRIFTED SHUT, momentarily blinding her to the New Orleans night sky, but making her aware in an altogether more intimate way. Though she couldn't actually see Ben kissing her neck with her eyes, she could too easily picture him in her mind, those beautifully sculpted lips leisurely sampling hers.

In her mind's eye, she could see those wonder-

fully masculine hands—hands that had so competently worked the sails this evening, powering
them out into this magical night—pushing into her
hair, kneading her scalp. Every nerve ending in her
body purred with pleasure and she could slowly
but surely feel her brain turning to mush right
along with her bones.

"God, you smell good," he murmured softly,
his voice a deep intimate drawl. "I haven't been
able to get you out of my head. I even dreamed
about you last night."

"Y-you did?"

"I did." He slid his hot tongue around the
shell of her ear, eliciting another shivering
quake. "I opened my back door and there you
were. You were wearing a long sheer gown…
with nothing underneath. I could see you, all of
you, and you were—" he let out a reverent sigh
"—stunning."

Mama mia, April thought. If this was what it
felt like to be charmed by *The Vagina Whisperer*,
then she was in for one helluva treat. Ben's voice
wound around her, lulling her cognitive senses
while masterfully inflaming others. They were in
their own little world—one of his making—embraced by a night backlit by stars and lights. And

true to his word, she wasn't cold. In fact, every particle in her being had warmed with startling rapidity.

"Did you dream of me?" he murmured, gently turning her head so that he could kiss her lids.

April nodded. "Mine are always waking dreams," she confessed. "I, uh… I had one in the car on the way over here."

Ben's chuckle vibrated against her lashes. "Good. I want you to think of me, to fantasize about me…and what I'm going to do to you."

April squirmed closer to him, framed his face with her hands and found his lips. The kiss was warm and languid, like the sound of his voice. His tongue pushed into her mouth, curled around hers—back and forth, back and forth—mimicking an intimate dance she longed to feel in her lower extremities. Extremities that were slowly but surely awakening beneath his expert touch.

Though she couldn't claim the deep throb of awareness that usually preceded an orgasm, she could feel a tingling warmth seeping into her sex. The seed of an orgasm taking root.

Ben deepened the kiss, then slowly drew her into his lap until she straddled him. She could feel the hot ridge of his arousal beneath her, settled firmly between her legs and the joy that bolted through her almost made her cry out.

What remained of her patience snapped and she rocked against him, desperate to feel the weight of his sex anchored deeply inside her. She didn't care if she had an orgasm on not. She just wanted to be as close to him as possible.

Ben clamped his hands on her hips, forcing her to still. "Patience," he whispered with a tortured laugh.

She tugged at the hem of his sweater, tunneled her hands beneath it until she found hard muscle and warm skin. Ben's belly quivered beneath her touch. She smiled against his lips. "I don't want to be patient."

"Rushing it isn't going to help you, babe."

Logically she knew that, but her body wasn't in agreement. In fact, her body burned.

It ached.

It needed.

But most importantly, it recognized that Ben was the one man who was going to be able to put her out of her misery, that he alone could lead her to the mountaintop, then cross over it with her.

"You came to me for help," he whispered softly, trailing kisses along her jaw. "Let me. Let *me* love *you*. Just let go. Stop trying so hard. It'll come. I promise."

Let me love you. Though she knew he didn't mean it literally—as in, emotionally—the words moved her all the same. Her silly heart melted and her resistance right along with it. Her taut-ened muscles relaxed and she slumped against him, content to let him…love her. He sighed softly and, for whatever reason, that gentle breath whis-pered over her soul.

Ben stroked her back. Lazily trailed his fingers alongside her spine, up and down. Straight lines, small circles, zigzags. "I love the way you feel in my arms," he said. "Soft. Supple. Womanly."

She loved the way it felt being in his arms. Se-cure yet dangerous, an odd combination for sure, but there was something slightly thrilling about it all the same.

His fingers gradually found their way back into her hair. He kneaded and massaged, swirled and rubbed, forcing her to relax, April realized. Mak-ing her aware of erogenous zones she'd never con-sidered. The small of her back, the curve of the hairline behind her ear. He was learning her, com-mitting to memory every response, and the idea that he was so thoroughly into what he was doing to increase her pleasure was intoxicating in and of itself.

Quite frankly, though she'd had a few decent lovers over the years, she'd never been with anyone who was interested in knowing her body well enough to customize their sex. It was the same-old same-old song and dance. Nipples, clit, nipples, clit, a little oral thrown in for good measure, then usually ten minutes of hot and heavy full-blown sex. Satisfying? Until eighteen months ago, yes.

But she highly suspected it wouldn't be anymore. Not after Ben.

This was the difference, April thought, as realization struck. *This* was how he'd earned his nickname.

He wrapped both arms around her, pressed her closer, then nipped lightly at her earlobe. Little lights danced behind her closed lids and the breath echoed out of her lungs.

Sweet mercy.

Now that had been done before, but evidently not correctly because she'd never felt a shiver hard enough to rattle her insides.

"Ah," Ben said, his voice low and intimate. "Now we're getting somewhere. Liked that, did you?"

"Y-yes."

"Then think of how much you'll like it when I'm inside you."

Her breath hitched, but before she could exhale, he caught it in his own mouth, kissing her deeply. God, he tasted good. Lingering champagne, sweet fruit and sharp cheese. A feast for the senses. April cupped his jaw, loving the way he felt beneath her palms. Smooth skin with a hint of masculine stubble.

Ben's hands had found their way to her waist, then moved upward in a slow trek that made her nipples pebble inside her dress. She shifted, hoping to push one aching breast into his palm and, though she felt the slightest hesitation—one that told her this, too, should wait—Ben's warm palm cupped her in a surrender that made her belly clench in a knot of delight.

She heard him swear softly, then he deftly moved the neck of her dress aside, shifting the fabric so that he could more readily feel her. His thumb found her nipple with alarming accuracy, snatching the breath out of her lungs.

He inhaled sharply. "No bra?"

"You said sexy," she reminded him. "FYI, I'm not wearing any panties, either."

"Christ."

April laughed. "Be patient," she mimicked, tossing the words back at him.

"Yeah, well, it's a helluva lot harder when I know the only thing that separates you from me is my zipper." He chuckled darkly. "FYI, I *never* wear underwear."

April drew back, inadvertently forcing his hand from beneath her dress, and stared at him. Oh, now that really wasn't fair. He was already torturing her, wasn't he? Wasn't she allowed any petty joy?

"They constrict," he explained, smiling, no doubt as a result of her shocked expression. "I like the freedom."

Freedom, hell. Now every time she looked at him she was going to know that he was going commando and it was going to drive her nuts. She'd be constantly scoping out his package—as if she didn't do that enough already, for Pete's sake.

"I'm liking it, too," April said. "Usually I wear thongs—same effect, almost—but this is…" She shifted above him and had the pleasure of watching his jaw clench. "…nice," she finished. "In fact, I like it so much, I'm going to propose a Rule Number Three."

Ben smiled and chewed the corner of his lip. His amber eyes twinkled in the moonlight. "Is that right?"

"It is. From this moment forward during Operation Orgasm, neither of us can wear underwear."

A startled laugh broke up in his throat. "Operation Orgasm?"

April smiled sheepishly. "Sorry," she said. "It's what a friend of mine is calling this mercy mission of yours. She's aware of my…problem, and has been hounding me for months to ask for your help."

Ben's head bobbed in a sanctimonious little nod. "Sounds like your friend is a smart woman."

"She is," April agreed.

His gaze tangled with hers. "But this is not a mercy mission."

"It is," she said. "But I don't mind." April's lips quirked. "How shameless is that?"

Ben considered her a moment, seemed to be weighing a decision of sorts. "Oh, hell, April. It's not shameless. The only difference between you and me is that you had the nerve to make the first move." She detected the smallest hint of self-disgust in that otherwise sexy voice.

She'd known that he'd wanted her—those hot

stares at the pub could hardly imply anything less—but she had to admit having him finally come clean about it was particularly gratifying.

"What happened to your nerve?" she asked, curious as to why he hadn't made a move.

Ben tensed, hesitated, then ultimately kissed the living hell out of her. She was out of breath, dazed and confused by the time he finally released her. "The answer to that would involve breaking Rule Number Two—"

Rule Number Two? Talking about their parents? April frowned. But—

"So, for the time being," he continued, "why don't we chalk it up to me being a perfect idiot and move on." He planted a kiss on her nose, then carefully helped her off his lap and stood. "We should probably be heading in. Wouldn't want to get hit by a barge."

Stunned, April felt her eyes widen. "Er…no. That wouldn't be a good thing."

Ben laughed. "Not if we want to live, no."

She nodded magnanimously, still bewildered by the Rule Number Two revelation and the abrupt subject change to barges and death. "I, personally, am in favor of living."

He smiled at her. "Good. I happen to be in fa-

vor of you living, too." He looked away, passed a
hand over his face, then found her gaze once more.
"My world has been a pretty boring place without you in it."

Since that was possibly one of the most beautiful things anyone had ever said to her, April decided to table the idea of pressing for more details
about Rule Number Two. It could wait....

At least until the end of the week.

Until then she planned to make the most of
rules one and three.

6

AH...NOW THAT WAS BEAUTIFUL, Ben thought, pulling the old antebellum home into focus. Seated about a hundred and fifty yards off the road, although he doubted there'd been one here at the time this old lady was built, the Picaine mansion had long ago been abandoned. Hard times, poor management. Who knew? But the end result was the same.

Something that had once been strong and lovely had been left to the ravages of time, uncared for, unlived in and unkempt. It was sad, a tragedy really, that the time, effort and care that had gone into building something so exquisite could be forgotten by later generations.

But despite the broken panes and sagging shutters, rotten boards and vandalism, there was still a beauty in the vulnerability of the architecture. That was what Ben liked to capture on film—the strength and nakedness of the old home. Left to their own devices, bushes, shrubs and trees had grown up around the old belle almost as if to embrace her, maybe hold her up.

Ben knew from experience that the odd clump of buttercups would bloom amid the underbrush in the spring, giving the lingering impression that someone had once cared enough to plant the bulbs. Other than a couple of woebegone cedar trees, there was nothing green, blooming or otherwise. It was bleak, melancholy, but still beautiful. It still reeked of *home,* even if it was a forgotten one. For whatever reason, Ben could identify with that. He could feel it, picking up certain vibes from older houses.

Working consistently, he framed a couple more shots, then made his way back to his car. A few detours later—he'd never been able to pass up an old dirt road since he'd found too many wonderful things waiting for him in the least likely of places—Ben finally arrived back at the office.

Hoping to avoid whatever business needed his immediate attention, he came in through the back entrance and quietly hurried into the lab. He wanted to develop these as soon as possible. He wouldn't know until he saw the film, of course, but that tingling excitement that heralded good work was whipping around his belly, spiking anticipation.

Unfortunately—hell, the woman had ears like a friggin' bat, Ben thought uncharitably—he hadn't even managed to take his camera out of the bag before Claudette knocked briskly at the door.

Ben muttered a curse. "I'm busy, Claudette," he said. "Whatever it is will have to wait."

"He's been waiting awhile already."

Ben tensed. Oh, shit. He knew who "he" was, but asked for confirmation anyway. "Who has been waiting?"

"Your father."

A litany of expletives hissed between Ben's teeth. He walked over and reluctantly opened the door. "How long has be been here?"

"An hour and a half."

"An hour and a half?" he parroted, astonished. "Didn't you tell him that you didn't know how long I'd be?"

Claudette nodded imperiously. "Several times."

"And he waited anyway?"

"He's quite determined to see you. Says he hasn't got anything else to do today."

Shit. Ben shoved his hand through his hair. "Does he know that I'm here now?"

She nodded. "He does. He saw you pull around back. When you didn't come through the front door, I think he assumed you'd seen his car and were attempting to further avoid him." Claudette paused, letting Ben fully absorb the guilt. "I corrected the assumption and made sure he understood your back-door entrance was a common occurrence." She paused again. "I am not making up any more excuses, Ben. I won't send him away. And I will not insulate you anymore. You're a grown man, for Pete's sake," she said, exasperated. "Act like one."

Ben shot her a stunned look. What the hell had happened to her? he wondered. Oh, he'd never had to wonder about her thoughts or opinions—particularly when it had come to his personal lifestyle or his father. A scowl of displeasure, a disapproving harrumph. But she'd never said anything so... So...honest, Ben realized.

Claudette shrugged. "From here on out, I'm speaking my mind. It's all part and parcel of the new me. Fire me if you don't like it. Otherwise, learn to cope." With a smile that could only be described as smug, Claudette turned on her heel and walked away. "Your father is waiting in your office. How long you leave him there is up to you."

Though he'd like nothing better than to go into his darkroom and explore his photos, or rethink every instant of last night with April—a frequent, make that constant occurrence since they'd parted ways at the riverfront—Ben pulled in a deep breath, let it go with a whoosh of dread, then slowly made his way down the hall to his office.

He opened the door and his father turned and stood. A ready smile, one that made a knot form in Ben's throat, sprang to his dad's lips. "Son," he said warmly.

Ben swallowed, strolled into the room and tried to pretend he hadn't been avoiding his father. He'd feel better behind his desk—needed the distance—but couldn't bring himself to do it. It was too disrespectful. "Sorry you had to wait so long. I was out at the old Picaine mansion today."

His dad inclined his head. "Beautiful place." He stroked his jaw. "Shame they let it fall to rack and ruin. Heart pine floors. No joints, either. If the room's twenty feet long, so's the board. Now that was craftsmanship."

Ben nodded. "It's a gorgeous place. I'm thinking I got several good shots out of it."

"Oh, I'm sure you did," his father readily agreed. He stared at some of the photos lining the walls. "You have a unique way of looking at things and an even better talent for capturing it." His dad glanced over at him. "I'm proud of you, Ben, even if you aren't of me."

Oh, hell. Ben passed a hand over his face. "Dad—"

"I heard that you're seeing April again," he said, swiftly interrupting him before he'd have the chance to deny it. Evidently Davy didn't want to force his son to lie, a fact that made Ben all the more uncomfortable.

"I'm glad to hear it," his father continued. "I've always thought she was the one for you, and I've always been sorry that I screwed it up for you."

"You didn't screw it up for me."

Davy smiled sadly. "I did, but it looks like you've got a second chance. Make the most of it."

Ben nodded, felt a smile twist his lips. "Morgana still got her spies in place?"

His father grinned. "A leopard doesn't change its spots. But the woman doesn't have the teeth or claws she used to have. She's on the rampage and she's bitter, but don't let her stop you. She certainly hasn't stopped April from being who she wants to be." A troubled frown pulled at his lips. "I wish Marcus would—" He stopped and drew up short.

Ben's senses hit red alert. "You wish Marcus would what?" he asked gravely.

Davy considered him, then with the relief of taking another into his confidence, he sighed. "I wish Marcus would tell her about me," he confided.

The floor beneath his feet might as well have rocked. "What do you mean tell her about you?" His eyes felt as if they were about to burst from their sockets. "You mean she doesn't know?"

"Not about me, no."

Ben swallowed uncomfortably. "But she knows that Marcus is—"

"—gay," Davy supplied with a small smile. "Yes. She saw him at a club we sometimes frequent last summer. Apparently she was hired to design their Web site and wanted to inspect it first."

So she'd found her father at a gay bar. That must have been awkward, Ben thought. "Wow," he said, for lack of anything better.

Davy's brows knitted. "She hasn't mentioned any of this to you?"

No. She couldn't because of Rule Number Two. He suddenly felt like a selfish ass. Shit. Shit, shit, shit. Distracted, Ben shook his head.

"It hasn't come up, no." He glanced at his father. "I can't believe Morgana hasn't told her."

Davy smiled. "Oh, don't think she wouldn't if April asked. But she's not going to as long as she can hold it over Marcus's head."

That sounded in character, Ben thought.

"No doubt you'll be hearing from her," his father commented. "I'm sure she's afraid that you'll tell her. And that would ruin her fun. She'd like nothing better than to come between April and her dad."

"If Marcus is avoiding her, then it sounds like she's already getting her wish."

Davy nodded. "I've pointed that out." He sighed. "For someone so smart, the man is certainly underestimating his daughter."

No doubt that was true, Ben silently concurred. Marcus ought to know that April wouldn't give a rip about who he was with. And frankly, unlike Ben, she'd probably be delighted that it was his father. She'd always adored him, had always talked about how lucky he was to have a dad who was good at "tinkering."

When he was growing up, his dad had helped them build tree houses and forts, had made spinning wheels out of old box fans. He'd shown them how to bait a hook, properly nurse a baby bird and plant a garden. He'd had a heart of gold and the patience of Job.

Ben glanced up at his father and for the first time in years, he noted the lines etched across his once-smooth face. And he saw more, as well. Worry and the fear of rejection.

His father wasn't weak at all, Ben realized. It took a helluva lot of courage to keep trying to love him when Ben had made it so damned hard.

"Well," his dad said. "I've taken enough of your time. I should let you get back to work." He turned and started toward the door.

"Dad."

Davy tensed and looked over his shoulder. "Yes, son?"

"Thanks for coming by." Ben cleared his throat. "It— It was good to see you."

A heartbreakingly hopeful smile tugged his father's lips. "You, too. Bring her by sometime, would you? I'd love to see her." He paused. "And I suspect someone else would, as well."

Ben watched him go, then settled behind his desk and tried to absorb everything that had just happened here. He'd learned that April didn't know about Marcus and his father—mind-boggling, that, he thought, still stunned—and, after all these years, he and his father had reached some sort of common ground. He didn't think he'd ever understand why his dad had made the decisions he'd made, but at least he could respect him for all the little things he'd taken for granted and, most importantly, never giving up on him.

Nevertheless, with this new information came a new problem—to tell or not to tell April. Clearly his father hoped he would, but Ben had trouble making it his place to do so, when clearly, Marcus wasn't ready for April to know. Did he think Marcus was wrong? Hell, yes. But that still didn't make it his place. Given that, he didn't know—

Claudette's knock sounded once more. "I really hate to bother you…"

"Ha!" Ben interrupted.

"…but there's a very unpleasant woman breathing down my neck who insists on seeing you," his secretary continued through uncustomarily gritted teeth.

Ben smiled. "Does she have horns and cloven hooves?"

White-faced and furious, Morgana Wilson nudged Claudette aside and stormed into his office. She planted her fists on his desk and leaned forward menacingly. "I thought I told you to stay away from my daughter."

"You did," Ben returned smoothly.

"Then what the hell do you think you're doing?" she quietly screeched.

Ben summoned a dark grin, one he knew would infuriate her. "Whatever the hell I want to."

"SAILING, EH?" Frankie asked. "Sounds romantic."

Seated at a corner table in Mama MoJo's, April smiled and filled her fork full of salad. "It was. I had no idea he was into sailing." Or into playing her body like a fine instrument, then finishing with a reverent kiss as the final note, as opposed to rocking her world with a hard orgasm.

But she knew it was coming and, after last night, looked forward to what he had in store for her next.

"Now tell me about these rules." Frankie grimaced. "Ugh. You know I detest rules."

Ordinarily, April did, too, but she was okay with his. She quickly filled her in and waited for her friend's response.

"I like the beck-and-call rule," she said, arching an interested brow—no doubt filing it away for her and Ross, April thought. "And the no-underwear rule is positively wicked. It means both of you are always ready, easily accessible. Open to one another." Frankie mulled it over. "That takes trust, more of it than you've probably realized." She aimed another shrewd look at her. "Are you sure you're not getting in over your head? I thought you just wanted him to fix your orgasm, then move on. This doesn't sound like a moving-on kind of relationship to me."

Honestly, April didn't know where she wanted it to lead. She hadn't thought that far in advance and purposely didn't want to—it wasn't part of her fantasy. Right now, Ben had been everything she could have possibly hoped for. Kind, enigmatic, sexy…and totally into her, which was an aphrodisiac in and of itself. She told as much to Frankie.

"What makes you think it's too personal?" she asked. Frankie had a way of seeing things that other people didn't necessarily. She was very perceptive, a trait April frequently envied.

Her friend smiled. "The combination of rules one and three attests to comfort levels and intimacy—but Rule Number Two suggests history." She cocked her head. "Wanna tell me the truth now, April?"

Trust Frankie to see past all the sex and seduction and get right to the heart of the matter. Ultimately, April summoned the nerve to confide in her, but it wasn't easy. There was something about sharing teenage heartbreak that made her feel juvenile and pathetic. Lots of people had teenage loves. They got over them. Clearly there was something wrong with her, because she'd just never been able to let it go. The wound had scabbed over, but it had never fully healed.

When she was finished spilling the whole sordid tale, Frankie sat in speculative silence for several minutes before speaking. "Your mother's a bitch."

April chuckled. "She is that."

Frankie hesitated, seeming to carefully weigh her words. "What you need to be asking yourself is why, babe," Frankie told her. "A woman doesn't get that bitter for no reason."

April snorted. "She doesn't need a reason to be bitter," she told her friend. "She's just…evil. Seriously. I can't imagine what my father ever saw in her that would propel him into marriage, much less how he ever got close enough to her to plant me." April paused. "I asked him about it when they divorced and he just shook his head and chalked it up to temporary insanity. Me, I think he knocked her up. I did the math," April said quickly, noticing Frankie's surprised expression. "I came seven months into their marriage. I guess he just couldn't *not* do the 'right' thing."

Frankie shrugged. "Bad luck there, but at least he's got you," she said.

Yeah, but there were times she wondered if that was compensation enough for what he'd had to put up with.

"So," Frankie said, interrupting her unpleasant thoughts. "What have you got planned for your beck-and-call session?"

"I don't know yet," April confessed. "That's why I wanted to talk to you. I thought you might be able to offer a few suggestions."

Back in her element, Frankie tapped a perfectly manicured nail against her chin. "Well, if you want to keep him, my advice is to take him to the voo-doo history museum and pick up a penis doll to show him what will happen to him if he is unfaith-ful."

Shocked at Frankie's typically outrageous sug-gestion, April whooped with laughter. Since last night, she hadn't been giving so much thought to keeping him as to making sure no one else had him. Arrogant? Selfish? You bet your sweet ass, but she couldn't help it. The idea of any other woman getting customized sex from Ben made her blood boil.

He was hers, dammit.

The thought of him taking the time to "learn" another woman and the joy that faceless whore would garner from his skilled touch made April's belly tip in a nauseated roll. The idea had been bad before, but now—particularly after last night—it was downright unbearable.

Frankie shrugged. "If you don't want to keep him, then any run-of-the-mill romantic gesture would be appreciated. Men are simple. Flash your tits at him and he'll pant like the dog that he is."

April giggled. Sweet Lord, how did Frankie come up with this stuff? Then another thought struck. "How do you know they have penis dolls at the voodoo museum?" April asked cautiously.

Frankie laughed. "How do you think I keep Ross in line?"

She snorted. "You're insane."

"For him," Frankie admitted with a long, reflective sigh.

"He'd never cheat on you, Frankie. He loves you."

"I know…but it never hurts to have a little added insurance." She propped her elbows on the table. "You'd be amazed at how effective it can be."

"What?" April gasped. "You've used it."

"Hell, yeah," her friend readily replied. "Let him look too long at some chick walking down the street and I pull that sucker out of my purse— along with a handy pair of scissors—and it's amazing how swiftly my baby remembers that he's only supposed to have eyes for me."

April clamped a hand over her mouth. "Oh, my God. You're serious!"

Frankie took a sip of her tea and smiled. "It's good for him to know how much I love him. Be- lieve it or not, I think he likes it. It just reaffirms that he's not alone in this crazy thing called love."

She could certainly see that, April thought. "I stand corrected. You are not insane—you are a genius."

Frankie sighed dramatically. "It's about time someone recognized my superior intellect."

"Consider yourself recognized," April said, still chuckling.

"I hate to do this to you," Frankie said, glanc- ing at her watch. "But I've got to bail. I haven't finished my column yet and it won't be long until Zora will be breathing down my neck. She's been in one funky mood lately," Frankie complained.

April frowned. "What do you mean?"

"One minute she's happy, the next she's weeping. She's coming in late, saying that she's having a hard time getting up in the morning. Then yesterday, I heard her puking her shoe soles up in her private bath. Hell, if I didn't know better I'd think she was—" Frankie's gaze widened and flew to hers.

April's heart had begun to pound and she felt a slow, disbelieving smile spread across her lips. "Pregnant," April finished, for once on the same page. "Oh, my God!" She leaned forward. "Do you think— Could she—"

Frankie snorted. "Hell, yeah. You know what that dirty poker is all about." A soft smile curled her mouth. "That's it," she murmured, her eyes aglow with something that remarkably resembled envy. "Zora's having a baby." Frankie quickly grabbed her purse. "I've got to go tell her."

April laughed. "My guess is that she knows."

"Then she's got some explaining to do, dammit," Frankie said. "Why the hell hasn't she told us?"

"You know how she is," April said. "Always playing her cards close to her vest."

"That or she just wanted to wait and see how long it took us to figure it out, the manipulative wench."

April cocked her head. "Ah… A more likely scenario."

Frankie turned to leave. "Call me and give me the lowdown on your beck-and-call session," she said over her shoulder as she made her way through the restaurant. "You know how I hate to miss anything."

April grinned, promising to keep her friend in the loop.

"And my money's on the penis voodoo doll," she bellowed, much to the shocked dismay of the occupants of the restaurant. Forks stalled at half-open mouths and several people swiveled their heads to look at April.

Oh, well, she thought, coolly sipping her drink. It was a good bet.

7

724 Rue Dumaine. Now.

Now, BEN THOUGHT, chuckling as he read the text message. Where did she get off with *now?* He'd at least given her an hour, the power-hungry witch.

He hit reply—a simple 10-4, then strolled out of the office. Or tried to.

"Where are you going?" Claudette demanded. "Have you taken a look at the initial designs for your Web site? Written any of the copy? Updated your bio?"

Ben paused, casting her a look that implied she worked for him, not the other way around. "Out, yes, no and no."

"Out," his secretary repeated, her brows arched. "Out where?"

Okay, Ben thought. There was definitely something up. Where was all this...this *lip* coming from? What the hell had happened to good old Claudette? "I'm meeting a friend." He frowned. "Is something wrong with you? Are you well?"

"I'm in perfect health. Why?"

"You seem different." He didn't know how old Claudette was, but he supposed she could be going through the change. He'd heard about other women going off the deep end when that happened.

She drew herself up behind her desk. "You mean because I've decided to quit biting my tongue and speaking my mind? Because I expect you to value me as a woman *and* as your secretary?"

"What?" Ben scoffed, flabbergasted. "I've always valued you, Claudette. Your Christmas bonus ought to tell you that."

"Money's easy, Ben," she sniffed. "From now on, I'm demanding respect."

Undoubtedly had he not clamped it shut, his jaw would have dropped. "Respect? You think I don't respect you?"

She shifted uncomfortably, but finally lifted her chin. "Most of the time, yes, but this is the new me, and since you're the man I spend the most time around, you're bearing the brunt of my anti-doormat training."

Antidoormat training? What the fu—

"My last three relationships have failed," she said, her voice throbbing with something akin to hurt. "You wouldn't know this because you've never been interested in my personal life. So long as I answer the phone and keep your office running like a well-oiled machine, you're happy. But you haven't noticed that I'm not. That's going to change, and it's beginning here. I'm a good worker. I deserve your respect."

At a complete loss, Ben set his hands at his waist and shook his head. Naturally he valued and respected Claudette. She was a crackerjack office manager. Her skill freed him up to do more in-the-field work and he truly appreciated that. Evidently, he hadn't done a bang-up job of letting her know it. Ben swore silently.

"Well, Claudette," he said with what he hoped was an appropriately contrite voice, "I am truly sorry that you have felt undervalued here." He cited her many attributes. "For what it's worth, I promise to make a concerted effort to be more—" he cleared his throat "—respectful."

She nodded primly. "Thank you. I would appreciate it." That settled, she promptly picked up the previous inquisition. "So you have looked at the initial design?"

"I have," Ben said. "Very impressive."

"I thought so, too, which is why I've been hounding you to get the copy to her. The sooner you finish, the sooner she can."

Yes, dammit, he knew that. But who had time to ready copy for April when he was too busy planning her seduction, contemplating Rule Number One and fantasizing about Rule Number Three. To think that she was somewhere in town right now waiting for him with no underwear on... Ben let out a broken breath.

Last night on the boat had been the mother of all exercises in restraint. The burning need, the all-consuming drive, to unzip his pants, lift her dress and bury himself to the hilt had been almost more than he could bear. Though he'd kept telling himself to be patient, that she deserved nothing less than the full-fledged seduction he'd put into motion, keeping his pecker in his pants was proving to be damned harder than he'd ever thought it would be.

He should have known better.

This was April, for chrissakes. He had a decade's worth of lust and longing built up. He couldn't simply turn if off now—or ignore it—just because he knew it was the right thing to do. That she deserved better.

Furthermore, to make matters worse, she was equally impatient. Had he been willing to move things to the next level last night, she would have been an eager participant. But despite the fact that he knew he could please her, intuition told him that the time was simply not right. She needed more wooing, more love.

Let me love you, he'd told her. Truer words had never been spoken. He wanted to love her with everything he had—heart, soul, mind. With every breath in his body, every last ounce of energy he possessed.

And to think that her bitch of a mother had thought that an angry visit would take that away from him. How gratifying it had been to thwart that mistaken assumption.

This time it was *he* who threatened to call the police and have her escorted from his premises if she didn't leave.

It was *he* who made her impotent with rage.

It was *he* with the power.

And it had felt damned good.

She'd played her trump card the first time she'd

warned him away. This time, she had nothing. Marcus had left her and moved in with Ben's father. And to be fair, Ben knew that Marcus had cared for his dad. When he thought about it, he supposed their relationship had lasted longer than any other he'd ever known.

In addition, April was no longer dependent on her mother for anything. She'd succeeded in getting out from under Morgana's thumb, making her own way—quite successfully, too, if her business was any indication.

Morgana had nothing…aside from a healthy fear that Ben would tell April about their fathers' relationship. If he had his guess, Morgana was waiting for Marcus to spill the beans—her first choice, he was sure because that would maximize his humiliation. And if that didn't happen, then she'd gleefully do it for him herself. Ben arriving on the scene definitely threw a wrench into her evil, vindictive plan…which explained her rabid anger this afternoon.

He mentally shrugged. Frankly, he liked being the fly in her ointment. Served her right for all the horrible things she'd said to him, the awful conclusions he had to live with all these years.

"So when are you going to get to the copy and

bio?" Claudette asked yet again. Geez, she was like a dog with a soup bone. What? Was she taking assertiveness training along with the antidoormat session?

Ben sucked in a breath. Respect, he reminded himself. "Tonight, possibly."

"But—"

His cell chirped at his waist with another message from April. *What? Was NOW not clear?*

What was with all these impatient women? He hit a quick reply, telling her he was on his way, then calmly informed Claudette that they'd have to continue this conversation later.

Thankfully Rue Dumaine wasn't terribly far from his office. He found a parking space, then started scanning address numbers until he found the right one. Or, what he suspected was the right one, Ben thought with an uneasy laugh.

The Voodoo Museum?

He checked her message again. Yes, it had said 724 and this was…724. A broken laugh erupted from his throat.

The door opened and April peeked her head out. "Are you going to stand out there all day, or are you going to come in?"

He looked up at the sign once more, casually

noted some of the displays in the windows on either side of the arched door. "Er...I guess I'm coming in."

April stepped forward, took his hand and tugged him inside. "Come on," she chided. "I've been waiting forever."

No doubt that was unpleasant, Ben thought, looking at a display of what appeared to be shrunken heads. "Sorry. *Now* wasn't doable." He paid their admission.

"And why not?" she asked loftily.

"Because my secretary has turned into a bossy marine in support hose," he said grimly. "We were having a discussion about 'respect'—or the lack of what she apparently thought she deserved," Ben clarified.

April looked away and her lips twitched with what he could have sworn was knowing humor, as though she was privy to some secret. "Do you treat her with respect?"

Ben shifted uncomfortably. He'd always thought so, but... "I treat her like an employee."

She led him into the *gris-gris* room. Bones, animal skin, dried herbs and small statues were displayed in various cases and attached to the walls. "How long has she worked for you?"

"She's been with me since I started."

April peered closely into a display case. "Oh. A long time then. When's her birthday?" she asked lightly.

Ben blinked. "What?"

"When's her birthday?"

He passed a hand over his face. Shit. "I, uh, I'm not sure."

"You've worked with her a minimum of six hours a day for the past—"

"—eight years," he said, reluctantly filling in the blank.

"Eight years, then, and you don't know her birthday?"

Well, when you put it like that… Ben thought, pretending to study a grisly voodoo doll. "Yes, well…"

April cocked her head, giving him a significant look, but thankfully let the subject drop.

"So," he said, relieved. "The Voodoo Museum. What brings us here?"

"Oh," April said, as though suddenly remembering the purpose for their visit. "I need to pick up a penis voodoo doll and I don't know your size."

PREDICTABLY, Ben's eyes bugged. "P-penis voodoo doll?" he choked.

"Yeah," April said, suppressing the almost
overwhelming urge to grin. "I had a chance to
look at them while I was waiting for you. It seems,
though, that they only come in one size, so technically, you didn't have to be here." Feeling distinctly wicked, she strolled out of the *gris-gris*
room into the hall.

Ben followed along behind her. "You're—" He
drew up short, waited for other visitors to pass by.
"You're buying a penis voodoo doll *for me?*" he
whispered gruffly.

She shot him a mysterious smile over her shoulder. "Given your nickname, I thought it would be
prudent."

"Prudent?" he repeated. "Why?" Ben pulled
her into another cramped room, then propelled
her around to face him. "Before you purchase a
doll for *me,*" Ben said, seemingly struggling to
take it all in, "I think we should discuss it."

April shrugged. "What's there to discuss? So
long as you don't wander off the straight and
narrow, I won't have to use it. For evil purposes,
at any rate," she added.

For the first time since she'd mentioned the doll,

Ben finally got past the shock of possibly having needles sticking in his figurative privates and considered the sentiment behind her impending purchase. He paused, considered her, and ultimately, his unnerved expression gave way to a shrewder one.

A slow smile slid across his lips. "Wander off the straight and narrow, eh? Does this mean you want exclusive rights to my penis?"

He sounded entirely too pleased with himself, April thought, biting the inside of her cheek. *Right again, Frankie.* "For this week, at the very least. Consider the doll insurance for anything beyond that until we see where this is going."

"If you dump me, can I have the doll?"

"Who's to say you won't dump me?"

Ben sidled closer, slid a knuckle down the side of her face. Those pale whiskey eyes pinned her to the floor, effectively sucking the air out of her lungs. "I can safely say that's one thing you don't have to worry about."

Wow, April thought, floored by the admission. Then, *wow* again, when those warm talented lips found hers. Sweet mercy. Ben's hands cradled her face, pushed into her hair and angled her head to deepen the kiss. It began reverent, a sweet offering, then quickly morphed into the kind of kiss that claimed ownership, demanded heat for heat, made her blood chug languidly through her veins, then race to her womb and warm her nipples.

In short order, he'd melted her heart, then set about incinerating the rest of her.

April wrapped her arms around his neck, pressed herself more closely to him. His scent, something mysterious and woodsy, wound around her senses, and though they were in a public museum in a room full of dark magic and dead things, April felt the seed of orgasm he'd planted last night grow into a tender sprout. Warmth pooled in her sex and a faint but definite throb had begun to beat steadily between her legs.

Evidently reading her mind, Ben shifted until his thigh was between her legs, an exquisite pressure that made her breath catch in her throat.

He dragged his lips away from hers, rained kisses along her jaw, then nuzzled next to her ear and nipped at her lobe while simultaneously pushing his thigh harder against her.

Pleasure barbed through her. Her neck weakened. Her toes curled.

Sweet heaven.

"I dreamed of you again last night," he murmured, rhythmically flexing his leg beneath her.

"Tell me."

Ben slid his hands over her rump, squeezed and growled low in his throat. She'd purposely worn a pair of rayon-spandex blend pants. No panty lines. "It was the same dream. You came to my back door. And you were wearing that long sheer white gown—a vintage one, I think, because at first I thought you were a ghost. I tried to talk to you, but you wouldn't answer me. You walked in, took my hand and led me to my bedroom." He laughed softly and she felt him nudge her belly. "From there it gets X-rated."

April leaned forward and sucked at his neck, pulling another deep growl of approval from his throat. "I'm of age. Do tell," she murmured suggestively.

Ben anchored his hands at her hips, pressed her more firmly against his leg, causing little flames of heat to flare in her loins. "You rocked my world," he said softly. "You stripped me, pushed me down onto the bed, then kissed, licked and suckled every part—and I do mean *every* part—of me. But you wouldn't let me touch you," he whispered roughly. "Every time I tried, you'd shake your head. I knew that if I disobeyed you, the dream would end, so I decided to enjoy letting you have your way with me."

April chuckled against his ear. "And that was such a hardship?"

"Oh, no. I loved every minute of it. *You* made love to *me*. Other than pumping into you while you rode me—your hair spilling over your shoulders, pouty nipples, sweet belly, oh, God—it was…effortless. I was the object of your lust and your only goal was to bring me pleasure. Trust me, babe. No hardship."

A wildfire raged in April's body as the image he'd just painted rose readily in her mind. She stilled, her breath coming in short puffs, as though what he'd described had just happened. Would that she could dream that way, April thought, envying him the sleeping fantasy.

Effortless, he'd said. She'd *taken* him. In his dreams, the master of seduction had been seduced himself. And it was to *her* that he'd given that power.

Heady stuff, that, April thought.

A feminine chuckle sounded in the background, bringing them back to reality. They slowly melted apart. "Now I see why you were interested in the penis voodoo doll," the curator murmured thoughtfully. She treated Ben to a leisurely inspection, then made a growling *mmm-hmm* sound of approval and nodded succinctly. "Were he my man, I'd have one, too."

To April's astonishment, Ben actually blushed. "She won't be needing one."

"Oh, yes I will," April said, moving toward the door. "I'm not taking any chances."

Five minutes later, much to Ben's scowling displeasure, she'd purchased the doll and secured it in her purse. They'd wandered around the corner to a local bar. The smell of draft beer and crawfish perfumed the air and the sound of slow jazz played from hidden speakers. They'd arrived at that quiet time between lunch and five, so other than the regulars, she and Ben were alone in the bar.

He took a pull from his longneck bottle of beer and idly nodded toward her handbag. "Now that would be an interesting object to explain to airport security."

April grinned. "I'm not planning on traveling any time soon."

"I can't believe you did that," he said, shaking his head.

She snorted. "I can't believe that I'm the only woman you've ever dated that has one."

He almost choked again. "What?"

"Come on," she needled. "You can't tell me that you haven't left a few broken hearts in your wake."

"Not intentionally."

"No one serious?"

Ben considered her a moment and that amber gaze tangled with hers. "One," he admitted. "It didn't work out."

"Sorry," she said, though it was a lie. If it had worked out, she and Ben wouldn't be here right now, wouldn't have that second chance. "What was the scoop on that relationship?"

Ben tipped his beer back. "She wasn't you."

This time, April almost choked. Her gaze flew to his. "Oh."

"What about you?" he asked. "Other than the guy who chased away your orgasm, has there been anyone else? One who got away?"

April shook her head, opting for complete honesty. "Nope," she said, releasing a heavy sigh. "You've always been the one that got away."

He bit his lip and a beat slid to three. "I'm still hooked, April. All you've got to do is reel me in."

8

"I FORBID YOU TO SEE HIM."

And that was the end of that conversation, April thought, disconnecting. Hanging up on one's mother was undoubtedly disrespectful, rude, even, but respect was earned and Morgana's supply had been depleted a long time ago. Any points she'd scored in raising April had been obliterated by her continued manipulative behavior.

In short, she was poison, and April had learned the antidote was removing Morgana from her world.

Predictably, her cell rang once more. A check of the display confirmed that it was her mother again. April heaved a put-upon sigh and reluctantly answered. "You can't forbid anything," April said matter-of-factly. "If you have something to say that doesn't pertain to my private life, then please continue. Otherwise, this conversation is over."

"Why, April?" her mother wailed madly. "Why? Of all the men in this city, in this part of the country, in the bloody world, *why* must you take up with that one?"

"Because I want to." Good grief, April thought. She'd expected some fallout, but this was over the top, even for her mother.

Looking back, April could understand her mother's feelings regarding her and Ben when she was younger—the close proximity, the intense feelings they'd shared for one another. For a parent hoping to keep her daughter's virginity intact, it was definitely a nightmare.

Curiously, though, April had never suspected that sort of motivation from her mother. There had been something entirely more...personal about it.

Frankly, even then April had gotten the impression that if she'd wanted to surrender her virginity to anyone *other* than Ben, it would have been fine. Her mother would have whisked her off to the gynecologist for birth control pills—no way in hell would she have trusted a boy to don a condom—and that would have been the end of it.

But it *had* been Ben then and it was Ben *now*. And the differences between then and now were ten years and April's blatant disregard for the woman who'd birthed her. Was she cold? Yes, probably. But Morgana Wilson was a high-maintenance, hard person to love.

Even her father, one of the kindest men April had ever known, had found it impossible.

"Can't you see that he's only doing this to get back at me? That he's thumbing his nose at me for running off his worthless hide the last time he came sniffing around you? For God's sake, April," Morgana said, thoroughly disgusted, "have some pride."

April felt her lips curl with angry humor. Like she'd said—*poison.* "I know this is hard for you to grasp, Morgana, but everything—"

"It's *Mother,*" she interrupted tightly. "I'm your mother, damn you."

April snorted. Morgana had lost the right to that title a long time ago. "—but everything," she continued doggedly, "is not about you."

"Mark my words," Morgana predicted smugly. "You'll be sorry. And when you are, I'll expect an apology."

Yeah. When hell freezes over, April thought. Hands shaking, she ended the call once more, then tossed the cell phone aside. If her mother called back, she simply wouldn't answer.

Now this was interesting, April thought, trying her best to get her mother's dire prediction out of her head. She wasn't speaking to her mother and her father wasn't speaking to her. Talk about dysfunctional.

Ben had told her yesterday afternoon that her mother had been by his office, so she'd expected a call. Honestly, she couldn't believe that her mother had abandoned the home front—she rarely ventured into public anymore, evidently the stigma attached to being a *divorced woman* was too much to bear—and had actually come to see him. Much to April's secret delight, Ben had sent her packing and had told her in no uncertain terms that he didn't have any intention of "staying the hell away from her."

Honestly, she didn't wish her mother any undue stress, but the woman needed to butt out of her business and stop trying to micromanage her. From the instant April had moved out from under Morgana's roof, she'd resisted all of her mother's attempts to manage her. Being able to make her own way had been the driving force behind getting her education and making her business a success. She'd be damned if she'd revert now, particularly to satisfy her mother's bizarre resistance to Ben.

Speaking of whom…if his little "I'm hooked" announcement over beers yesterday afternoon had been any indication, he definitely wanted to continue things beyond this week. In fact, what he'd actually said was "I'm *still* hooked" which implied that, like her, he'd never gotten over their relationship, either.

April couldn't claim that they'd picked up right where they'd left off. They were older, more mature. Back then, their dates had consisted of church hayrides and stolen trips to the river, picnics and sitting on the front porch. Other than her mother's habit of casting a pall over everything, they'd had little to worry about. They'd focused every bit of their attention on one another and the future they'd hoped to have.

Now there were deadlines and insurance, cable bills and past relationships. With maturity had come reticence, particularly, she knew, on her own part. The thing was… Ben had been her hero, her knight in shining armor. It had been too much to foist upon a teenage boy, she knew now. And the best part about becoming an adult had been learning she could save herself.

But that didn't help assuage the prick of hurt that still smarted, even after all these years.

Though she knew it was unreasonable—and though she *hated* her mother for saying it—a small part of her worried that she would be sorry. That she'd embrace the opportunity for a second chance and something else would go wrong.

That's why, for the moment at any rate, she planned to continue practicing self-delusion and tell herself that it was all about the sex, that these sweet, heartwarming aspirations Ben kept casting upon their future together were just part of her customized, tricked-out seduction.

He'd called her bright and early this morning, before she'd even rolled out of bed, and had asked her to spend the day with him. He was working in-the-field and would like her to come along for the ride. The ride, she'd finally gotten out of him, was literally a ride. Ultimately, he explained, this was how he worked. He got into his car and drove around, weaving in and out of back roads until he found a subject that struck his fancy.

This sounded like something they would have done in the past so she'd been inordinately pleased that he'd asked. She'd called Margo and Joyce and given them the heads-up that she wouldn't be in today, then dressed in something warm and comfortable.

Ben was loading up his SUV with various camera accessories when she pulled into the small
parking lot behind his office. He looked up and
smiled when he saw her, making her heart do an
odd little pirouette.

She walked over and peered into the back of his
vehicle. "What's with the picnic basket?"

"You'll wanna eat, won't you?"

"Do I look like I miss a meal?"

Ben settled his rear against the back of the
open hatch, grasped her hand and tugged her forward until she leaned fully into him. Hot goose
bumps erupted on her skin and a sigh of pure
contentment seeped past her lips as she looped
her arms around his neck and met those twinkling
smooth whiskey eyes.

"You look like lunch to me," he said suggestively, "but I figured you might get hungry."

"Oh, I'm sure I could find a little something to
munch on," she said coyly.

His eyes widened with masculine outrage. "A
little something?"

April threw her head back and laughed. "Sorry.
I didn't mean to insult little Ben."

"Little again." He gave his head a lamenting
shake. "You're hard on a guy's ego."

April batted her lashes shamelessly. "Thank you. I try."

Ben reluctantly helped her stand. "Yeah, well. We need to work on you setting some new goals." He threaded his fingers through hers. "Come on," he said. "I need to tell Claudette that we're leaving."

April followed him through a back door and down a long hall. Finally they reached the lobby area she'd waited in that first day she'd come to his office. Once again she was struck by the masculine elegance of the office.

Claudette looked up as they approached. "Good morning," she said.

"I just wanted to let you know that I'm heading out," Ben said. "I'll have my cell, but don't count on it having service."

Seemingly pleased, his secretary nodded. April felt her lips twitch. Evidently Ben taking off to parts unknown without having the courtesy to let Claudette know where he was going had been a problem. No more, it would seem, April thought, pleased with both his effort and Claudette's improving self-worth.

Though Ben was not privy to it, April knew exactly what had gotten into Claudette—Chicks In Charge.

When Ben had mentioned that April was going to design his site, Claudette, good secretary that she was, had visited April's own Web site, inspected several of her designs—like Chicks In Charge, for instance—and had e-mailed various clients, asking if they were happy with April's work.

Evidently the Chicks In Charge site had piqued Claudette's interest and within a matter of hours, April had given the woman her own personal testimonial as to what the organization had done for her. Claudette had attended a chapter meeting the night before last and the rest, as they say, was history.

"If I don't see you before you come back, I'll put your messages on your desk," Claudette told him.

Ben thanked her, then looked at April. "You ready?"

"Sure."

"All right then." He found her hand once more, the gesture unwitting and uncalculated, as though he merely wanted to touch her, then propelled her back toward the hall.

April shot a look over her shoulder at Ben's secretary. "Bye, Claudette."

Claudette winked at her. "Goodbye, Ms. Wilson."

Ben had turned just in time to see Claudette's silent message. He frowned down at April as they retraced their steps down the hall. "What was that all about?"

"What?" she asked innocently.

"She winked at you."

"She did? I hadn't noticed."

He cocked his head. "She winked. I saw her."

April shrugged. "She might have had something in her eye."

Still looking adorably confused, Ben stared at her for a few seconds longer, then shook his head and muttered something that sounded suspiciously like "women."

Looking sleek and beautiful in her shades, April sat in the passenger seat next to him, her small hand enfolded loosely in his. "Are you having a good time?"

They'd been at it for a few hours, driving aimlessly, stopping every once in a while for him to frame a few shots. He'd even convinced her to let him take a few of her. Honestly, people had never been quite as inspiring to him as architecture, but something about April in particular made his fingers itch to capture her on film.

She turned her head to face him. "Yeah, I am. This is very interesting. I had no idea all of these old structures were out here."

He negotiated a turn. "Most people don't." He lifted a shoulder in a negligent shrug. "Personally, I enjoy looking for them as much as I enjoy finding them."

She shot him a grin. "Yeah. I'd noticed that." She paused. "Seriously, it's fascinating. And you are very good at what you do."

For whatever reason, her respect and approval meant more than he would have ever thought possible. He nodded, trying to think of something witty to say, but found himself unable to come up with anything. He settled for a simple thank-you. "You're good at what you do, too. Did I tell you that I looked at the initial design you'd sent me?"

"No," she said, turning to face him again. "I'd wondered what you'd thought about it."

She would see shortly, Ben thought, fighting a small smile. "It's fantastic. The shot of that live oak as the background is perfect. I would have never thought to use it, and yet it captures the tone and variety of my work perfectly." He nodded. "Very discerning of you."

"I thought so," she said, seemingly pleased with the praise. "I kept coming back to it." A puzzled line emerged between her delicate brows. "It's very compelling...and it reminded me of you."

He laughed. "Me?"

"Yep. Dark and forbidding. Vulnerable but strong. Peaceful, even."

He liked dark, forbidding and strong. He could tolerate peaceful, but drew the line at vulnerable. "What makes you think I'm vulnerable?" he asked suspiciously, shooting her a sideways glance.

She laughed softly and shook her head. "I knew you'd call me on that one."

She neatly avoided answering it, too, but Ben wasn't ready to let her off the hook. "Come on. What makes you think I'm vulnerable?"

"I can't tell you."

"Why not?"

April sighed, gazed out the window. "Rule Number Two."

Since Ben didn't particularly care for that answer and what it implied, he decided to ignore her response. Honestly, he'd like to tell her about the understanding he and his father had reached, but doing so would violate Rule Number Two, and furthermore, he could hardly talk about his own father without telling her that Davy was her dad's partner.

Sticky stuff. Dangerous waters.

He had a horrible fear that his silence on the matter would come back to bite him on the ass, but he couldn't get past it really—*really*—not being his place. It was Marcus's place. Marcus should tell her, dammit, and if things progressed between him and April the way he hoped they would, Ben wasn't above paying her father a visit to give him his opinion on the subject. He wasn't certain it would do a whole hell of a lot of good, but he'd give it a try nonetheless.

April deserved her father's honesty and in the meantime, it put him at a dishonest disadvantage by creating this lie of omission between them. He didn't like it.

In fact, it sucked.

"Are you getting hungry?" Ben asked at last, when they neared the place where he'd planned to stop and picnic.

April stretched a bit in her seat. "Yeah, I'm getting a little hungry."

He heaved a put-upon sigh and smiled. "Back to the little jokes, I see."

She chuckled. "You know what I mean," she chided. "Geez, who would have ever thought you would be so sensitive? For someone whose nickname is *The Vagina Whisperer,* of all things, you sure are insecure."

Ben rounded another turn and the great tree he'd photographed years ago—the very one April had said she'd been drawn to—came into view. He slowed, watched her from the corner of his eye and waited for her to see it.

"Oh, wow," she breathed, her gaze widening with delight. "Would you look at that? That looks like—" She glanced at him questioningly, a wondering smile curling her lush mouth. "Is that what I think it is?"

He grinned.

"Oh, Ben," she said, her voice soft with emotion.

"I thought you might like to see it."

She leaned over and brushed a kiss against his cheek, causing something in his chest to shift, tingle and quake. "So that's what the picnic basket's for?"

"Good surprise, eh?"

She nodded. "Excellent surprise." She kissed his cheek again, then leaned up and tugged at his earlobe with her teeth, causing his belly to tremble and a shiver to race up his spine. "I'll be sure and reward you accordingly," she growled softly.

Ben pulled off the road. She didn't get it yet, did she, he thought, shifting the gearshift into park. He turned in his seat and ran the pad of his thumb over her bottom lip. For the briefest of seconds, he laid himself bare to her, let her glimpse the emotion keeping him in a perpetual knot. "Just being with you is reward enough," he said.

And he meant it.

April's gaze softened. "Ben," she breathed, then leaned forward and kissed him ever so gently. "I don't know what to say."

"That's the beauty of it," he said. "You don't have to say anything." He drew back. "Come on. What do you say we go spread the blanket and share a bottle of wine?"

Her eyes twinkled. "I say yes."

Ben got out and retrieved the basket, while April snagged a couple of blankets. His arm slung around her shoulder, they made their way across the dry brown field until they reached the slightly chilly shade of the tree.

"It's gorgeous in the spring," Ben told her. "I've taken shots of it then, too, but it's just not as compelling, if that makes sense." He set the basket down, then took one of the blankets from her and spread it on the ground. The other, he set aside.

"It does," she said, looking up, admiring the knotty canopy overhead. "When she's dressed, you can't see her branches."

Ben cocked his head. She was right, but he still wanted to tease. "So you're saying I like her better when she's naked?"

April grinned. "I didn't say it, hoss, you did." She sank down onto the blanket. "Seriously, the branches, the breadth of the tree, I think that's what makes it so beautiful."

Ben settled down beside her, poured her a glass of wine, then went about loading their plates. Cajun chicken salad, marinated vegetables, fresh fruit and a carrot-raisin muffin to start, then bread pudding with warm rum sauce to finish.

April grinned at him. "Now this is what I call dinner on the ground."

Ben shot her a look. "I've got a different definition. I'd be happy to show you later, if you're interested."

April's chewing slowed and a smile rolled around her lips. "Oh, yeah. I'm interested."

They ate in comfortable silence, embraced beneath the towering shade of the tree, cozily enveloped in her bare branches. When April had finished, Ben loaded everything back up into the basket, then lay down and tugged her with him, snagging that extra blanket in the process. She settled her head upon his chest, seemingly content to listen to his heart beat. He covered her up, equally content to let her.

After a moment, she lifted her head and peered up at him. "Thank you," she whispered softly, her voice rusty with emotion.

"For what?" He painted circles on her back with his fingers. Contentment welled inside him, affirmed what he already knew in his heart to be true.

"For this. For everything."

"I haven't fixed you yet," he told her.

"You have in every way that counts," she replied, her gaze searching his. She scooted up and kissed his jaw, causing a tornado of heat to rush into his loins. "I'm ready," she whispered huskily.

Ben let go a shuttering breath. "Ready for what?"

He knew, dammit, he knew. Knew what she wanted and why she'd come to him to give it to her. But for whatever reason—performance anxiety, he supposed—he was suddenly an absolute nervous wreck. He'd done this countless times. And he knew that she was ready. He'd primed her. Awakened her senses, put her back on the path of sexual healing.

And yet, now that the time had come to work his magic, he was suddenly terrified of not pleasing her. Of being just like every other guy over the past eighteen months who'd left her tired but not satisfied.

It was damned intimidating to say the least.

"That dinner-on-the-ground definition you mentioned earlier," she said, confirming his fears.

Sweet Jesus. *Him.* Ben Hayes, the freakin' *Vagina Whisperer*, was afraid of having sex. He stilled.

Fuck that, Ben thought, as ego and pride quashed the intolerable notion. In a nanosecond, he bent his head, captured her lips and every insecurity vanished like dew in the Louisiana Delta.

April *would* come for him because failure was not an option.

And neither was losing her again.

9

APRIL SENSED more than felt the abrupt change in Ben. A confidence and urgency entered his kiss, even his touch as he pulled her up over his body. He slid his hands along her back, shaping her, pressing her more firmly against him.

Oh, have mercy, she thought, as equal parts joy and desire bolted through her. Her blood sizzled in her veins and a warm, tender feeling infected her heart, causing her to smile against his lips.

After little more than three days, Ben had managed to coax feeling back into her numbed sex, and insinuate himself back into her heart. Hell, who was she kidding? For whatever reason, she was reminded of one of those grow-your-own-boyfriend kits, the kind where you only had to add water and a tiny sponge would morph into a life-size man.

Ben had been like that—there, but small…dormant. But the instant she'd invited him back into her life, he'd somehow managed to grow and swell until her heart could no longer deny that she was, is, and always would be head over heels in love with him.

And this afternoon, under a tree—the very tree that she'd fantasized about being with him beneath, one that had weathered hurricanes and droughts and had most likely given shelter to Confederate soldiers—he was finally going to make love to her.

Let me love you.

Oh, she intended to. But she would match him pleasure for pleasure because she had every intention of loving him, too. And given the dream he kept having, she knew that he wasn't used to it.

"Do you have any idea how long I've waited for this?" she asked him.

"You said eighteen months."

"No," she said, bracing both hands on either side of his head. She peered down at him, bent and kissed his lids, then the side of his cheek, then slid her tongue along his bottom lip and suckled him gently. "Eighteen months is how long I've waited for an orgasm. I've waited for you—for this—for ten years," she told him. "Ten long, lonely years."

Masculine approval flared in those amber orbs. "You haven't been alone."

She bent and tasted him again. "No more wasted time."

Ben smiled, nodded, then swiftly rolled her over onto her back. "As you wish," he murmured in a husky voice that bordered on a growl. He settled himself alongside her body, and attached his mouth to hers once more, then slowly slid his hand under her shirt. She gasped and her belly quivered beneath his warm touch. He trailed his fingertips around her navel, then played her ribs like a harp, painstakingly strumming each one until her nipples tautened into hard aching nubs that she longed to push into his hand.

With every sweep of his tongue into her mouth, every slide of his fingers over her body, she could feel her muscles thaw and throb, melt and quiver. Much to her delight and irritation, he seemed to be taking his time, intent on stoking a fire that was already lit.

You'll come for me, then I'll take you, and you'll come again.

That sure as hell looked like a promise he planned to make good on, April thought, resisting the wild urge to laugh.

Desperate to feel something besides her own pleasure, April tugged his sweater up and breathed a sigh into Ben's mouth when she found warm, bare skin. God, the man felt wonderful. Smooth skin, supple muscle, a feast for her palms. Slowly, deliberately, with the same sort of painstaking care he was using, April worked his sweater up until he had to break their kiss in order to push it over his head. With a flick of her wrist she tossed it away, then quickly smoothed her hands down his sides.

His breath caught and she felt him—*him,* big fearless, experienced him—quiver. A rush of power ripped through her, causing her own breath to stall and break. A steady, promising pulse had begun to pound in her sex and warmth pooled in her womb, watering the sprout of the orgasm he'd planted over the past few days. With every beat of her heart, she could feel it getting stronger, growing, the bud forming…the promise of a bloom.

Ben gently removed her sweater and tossed it carelessly aside. He stilled and fingered her bra, a sheer pastel butterfly design. The delicate gauzy wings covered her breasts. "Pretty," he murmured.

April smiled wickedly. "I have the panties to match…but I'm not wearing them."

Ben chuckled, and quickly popped the front closure on her bra, causing the wings to break apart, the fabric to snag on her pebbled nipples. He bent and nudged the sheer material aside with his nose, then licked her nipple, blew, then suckled.

A pleasure so sweet and intense forced her lids to flutter shut. Her head rolled languidly to the side and she mewled softly, a nonsensical confirmation of his expertise. She slid her hands into his hair, anchoring him there, then arched off the blanket, pushing her aching breast farther into the hot cavern of his mouth.

Ben's hand found her other breast. He weighed and thumbed, lightly squeezed, then evidently wanting to see if there was a difference between them, he licked a path over and quickly pulled her neglected nipple deep into his mouth. She felt that hot tug in her womb, as well, as though a mysterious thread connected the two. Every stroke of his tongue, every suckle, vibrated it until she genuinely feared she'd fly apart.

Oh, sweet Jesus, April thought as he took his sweet time torturing her. She knew what he was doing—he was loving her—drawing out the pleasure, building, stoking, kindling. And in the meantime, she was burning up inside. Her skin seemed entirely too tight for her body and she was hit with the simultaneous urge to stretch and purr, squirm and wiggle.

They were overdressed, she decided, and quickly went to work at the snap of his trousers. She'd barely touched the zipper when she felt him jump, an impatient nudge that told her he was every bit as ready as she was. Three seconds later, she had him in her hand, hot, hard, thrilling.

Huge.

Perhaps The Vagina Invader was a better nickname, April thought with an inappropriate burst of humor as she stroked the slippery skin with her hand, ran the pad of her thumb over the smooth, engorged head.

Ben sucked in a harsh breath and swore hotly. "Christ, April."

"I love touching you," she said, skimming the tips of her nails over him, then slipping her hand down to gently cup him.

With a groan that told her it cost him, Ben pulled himself out of reach, shucked his sagging pants, then made quick work of hers.

Naked, at last, she thought with a shuddering sigh as Ben's hot skin connected fully with hers.

He fed at her breast again, then slowly trailed his fingers down her belly. April felt her thighs quake, anticipating what would come.

Namely her…soon.

As though his shoulders weren't shaking and he had all the time in the world, he drew a lazy M over her pubic bone, dipping down, tantalizing her clit, then up again. A shock of moisture coated her folds, drenched her, from the teasing contact.

April whimpered. "Ben," she pleaded. "Enough. Please."

He chuckled softly, the sound dark and wicked… Her bad boy. "You're almost there." He drew another lazy M, dipping down farther this time, dragging some of her joy juice up and painting it over her pulsing nub once more.

She bucked off the blanket, shamelessly opened her thighs more, granting him better access. Open, ready, desperate. She felt his breath pool in her belly button, his tongue slide in a direct path where his fingers played, then with an uncustomary burst of speed, he quickly latched his mouth upon her.

Oh. Sweet. Heaven.

Her eyes rolled back in her head. What little air had been in her lungs swiftly departed in a startled whoosh, and had he not wrapped his arms around her legs, she would have bucked him off her. Instead, Ben held her down and tongued her harder.

"Oh, baby, you taste good."

She couldn't speak, couldn't reply.

"Sweet... Hot..."

He licked and stroked, swirled and massaged, his tongue every bit as adept as his fingers. April gasped. Maybe more so, she thought as, blessedly—oh, God, *finally*—she felt the sweet tug of beginning climax. Ben loosened his hold upon her legs, let his fingers drift into the fray. He tongued her clit, lapped and laved, then slipped his thumb deep into her and squeezed, pushing his index finger against the tight rosebud of her bottom.

It was beyond anything she'd ever experienced before. The air evaporated from her lungs, a silent "oh" tore from her throat, her thighs went rigid. He pulled another neat trick with his tongue, forming a stiff V over her clit and working it back and forth, back and forth, and all the while his thumb and finger kept perfect harmony.

April thrashed beneath him, could feel the climax bearing down on her, tightening and tightening until with one final push against her bottom, the dam broke and a year and a half's worth of orgasms burst free.

She cried out—screamed—then laughed hysterically with relief as the pleasure pulsed through her. Ben kept up his ministrations, but slowed them down enough to let her get the most from the experience—let her savor it rather than fight it.

At last, when the final throb echoed away and nothing but a tingling warmth lay in the aftermath of release, he looked up at her. Masculine pride— the baby-I-rocked-your-world kind—clung to his smile. Those pale whiskey eyes were dark with desire and twinkled with just the smallest bit of smug humor. "Welcome back," he murmured, intensely pleased with himself.

April grinned at him, leaned forward and pulled him toward her so that his sex nudged hers. Her hips lifted in silent invitation. "Welcome *in*."

IF SHE EXPECTED HIM to dive in and take his own pleasure without making sure that she got even more, then she'd better think again, Ben thought, resisting the urge to draw back and beat his chest and roar.

Granted, his dick throbbed and his arms were shaking. Even though every single part of him was ready to fly apart the instant he allowed it, Ben knew that she still needed something more. Something better. Something just for her. Hell, if he didn't come at all—though, quite honestly he hoped that wouldn't be the case since it would likely kill him—it simply wouldn't matter.

She'd come. For him.

Right now, all past and future accomplishments didn't mean shit.

Because he'd been right. Her libido had gone into hibernation, waiting for the right guy. It had rebelled against mediocre lovers and men who didn't truly care for her, waiting for him. *For him, dammit.* And while he'd milked the first climax out of her, he knew there were many more to come.

And he had every intention of making another one appear soon.

Though the restraint was killing him, though his entire body was racked with the need to bury himself to the hilt inside her, Ben drew back a hairbreadth and slid deliberately between her hot, slicked folds, bumping her still-sensitive clit.

"Oh-h-ho," she laughed, pushing up against him. "That's cruel. You know I want you inside me."

Ben bent and sucked a rosy nipple into his

mouth, the taste of her exploding on his tongue. God, how he loved her body. It was small and compact, making heaven a mere nod away. She was smooth, soft and firm, a breathtaking combination of sweet curves, intriguing valleys. Pale skin, dark curls, dusky nipples. Her hair fanned out on the blanket, a mass of sexy, gorgeous curls.

She was, in every sense of the word, perfect.

"And I want to be inside you," he told her, moving to the other plump breast. "But you must have pa—"

"Patience," she finished, seemingly ready to howl. "I came," she said, very *im*patiently. "It was magnificent, glorious, amazing. But I want you to fill me up. I'm hollow and achy and—" she rocked her hips forward burying the head of his penis inside her "—I *need* you."

She leaned forward and nipped at his neck, causing a shower of sensation to trickle over his skin. She lifted her hips once more, pulling him even farther into her body, then she sank back as if the pleasure were sapping her energy.

It was one of the most erotic things he'd ever seen. Need, desire, want…they were bleeding her strength, leaving her boneless with yearning, a willing love slave, enthralled and bound to him.

Ben drew back and slid between her pink folds once more, then dipped into her. Instinctively her feminine muscles clamped around him, attempting to trap him, draw him in. His dick throbbed with pleasure and he felt the beginning tingle of climax stir in his loins.

He dipped again, this time lingering a moment before withdrawing, savoring the feel of her wet heat fisting hard around him.

April's neck bowed, exposing her delicate throat, and her mouth opened in a silent moan of ecstasy. She arched beneath him, lifted her hips and rocked, then slid her hands up over his belly, grazed his midsection and scoured his masculine nipples with those neat, manicured feminine nails.

Talk about a turn-on.

He shuddered, closed his eyes, and only by sheer dint of will did he manage *not* to collapse on top of her, to push himself so far into her that it would take Jaws of Life to get him out.

He pushed again, this time surrendering, and buried himself deeply inside her. A sublime smile of satisfaction curled her kiss-swollen lips and her lids drifted shut beneath the weight of pleasure.

Seeing her reaction, feeling the absolute flawlessness of being inside her, made Ben's eyes drift shut, as well.

She was… She was… Words failed him. There was no way to aptly describe the matchless perfection being inside her inspired in him. His throat clogged, his heart raced and, were his toes not firmly planted into the blanket, they would have undoubtedly curled. A whirlwind of sensation—both physical and emotional—caught him up and spun him until he didn't know anything beyond the brilliance of this moment.

April clamped around him again, rocking her hips, a silent but effective request and, because he wanted nothing more than to lie beneath this tree and make love to her for the rest of his life, he set everything else aside and concentrated on giving her that second orgasm he'd promised her.

With a deliberate flex, he withdrew and plunged into her again. Finding a slow rhythm, he savored the resistance, the perfect draw and drag of their joined bodies. She drew her legs back and anchored them about his waist, then reached around and cupped his ass with her warm hands, squeezing, urging, a mewl of carnal pleasure, a purr of satisfaction. She matched him thrust for thrust, easily, as though they'd done this thousands of times, finding his pace, keeping it, then demanding more.

He felt her tighten around him, then her voice caught, and she upped the tempo. She sank her teeth into her bottom lip, whimpered and thrashed, the fever driving her mindless. Whereas seconds ago she'd been boneless and limp, now she'd gone rigid and wild, desperate for the second orgasm Ben firmly intended to serve up.

His own loins were experiencing the fiery torments of the damned and every cell in his body was ready for release. The instant she caught hers, Ben knew he'd come.

He wrapped an arm around her waist, pushing her back even farther, then pumped frantically, pistoned in and out of her until he thought for sure that his heart would explode. Her feminine muscles clamped again, heralding her impending climax. Breathing raggedly, Ben smiled, then leaned forward, licked the shell of her ear and then deliberately nipped at her lobe.

Predictably, she shattered.

A long keening cry tore from her throat. Her body bowed off the blanket, bucking beneath him and the walls of her channel clenched forcefully around him.

And that was all it took to make him detonate like a nuclear bomb, pleasure imploding upon itself. She spasmed hard around him, flexed and quivered, and with each pulse he felt himself quake inside her. Her climax perfectly milked his, draining him of everything but the sublime satisfaction of phenomenal sex.

When the very last pulse throbbed out of him, Ben gently withdrew, then collapsed beside her and rolled her next to his side. He tucked the blanket firmly around them. Her head lay nestled against his chest, her curls spilling over, tickling his side. She rested her fingers upon his belly, and slung a smooth leg over his thigh. In short, she melted over him like hot fudge over a scoop of ice cream and he didn't know when he'd ever felt anything more amazing in his life.

Her. Him. Here.

Heart still pounding, Ben bent and kissed the top of her head, looked up at the canopy of branches and felt a wash of contentment bathe his soul. The sun had begun its descent, painting the fall sky in a glorious display of color.

"Ben?"

He doodled on her upper arm. "Yes."

"I've got a confession to make."

He smiled against her hair. "Yeah? What's that?"

She let go a soft whispering breath and nuzzled closer to him. "I'm still hooked, too."

His chest tightened, forcing him to swallow. Good, he thought. He could hardly wait to reel her in.

10

"I STILL CAN'T BELIEVE that you kept something like this from us," Frankie griped. "You're pregnant, for Pete's sake. You don't think you could have mentioned that?"

Zora lifted a cool shoulder and idly sipped her virgin margarita. "I wanted to get past my first trimester before telling you guys. You know, in case something went wrong."

Slightly mollified, Frankie nodded.

"We understand," April said. They usually met at the Blue Monkey on Friday nights, but in light of everyone having—or at least everyone with exception of Frankie—good news to report, they decided to get together for a celebratory meeting. No bitchfest tonight, April thought, with a soft smile.

A rare smile curled Carrie's lips. "Well, we're thrilled for you, at any rate," she announced. "You'll be a fantastic mama."

Zora grinned. "And the three of you will make equally fantastic honorary aunts."

"What did Tate say when you told him the news?" April asked.

"You told *him* before the end of your first trimester, didn't you?" Frankie interrupted. "Because if you didn't that's just—"

"I told him," Zora said, fondly exasperated.

Frankie nodded succinctly. "Well, good."

"He's thrilled," Zora reported. "A nervous wreck, but thrilled."

April could certainly see that in Tate's character. Much like Ben, Tate was a he-man kind of guy, the type who took the whole "love and protect" thing very seriously. Adding a child to the mix had to be disconcerting, but she didn't have any qualms that he wouldn't be anything short of a fantastic father. This was going to be one lucky baby, April thought, slightly envious of their budding family.

For the first time in her life, she heard the tick of her biological clock, felt a yearning for her own family. An amber-eyed, dark-haired baby sprang to mind. Her lips quirked. It was definitely telling that she'd given her imaginary offspring Ben's features.

Finished with her turn in the hot seat, Zora

swirled a straw around her drink and looked at Carrie. "Well," she said. "I understand that you have some news to report, as well."

Carrie smiled self-consciously. "Nothing as remarkable as having a baby," she admitted. "But I did get some good news this week."

"Do tell," Frankie murmured, happiest when juicy tidbits were forthcoming.

Carrie dragged in a small breath. "I was offered my own show."

She'd suspected as much, but April whooped with joy nonetheless. A round of raucous applause rang from their table, causing the few other patrons in the bar to shoot them a glance.

"Carrie, that's fabulous!"

"You bet your sweet ass it is," Frankie enthused in her typical blunt fashion.

"Congratulations," April told her. "When do you start?"

"Wait!" Frankie interrupted. "First things first—have you told Martin yet?" Martin—better known as the dickless wonder among their set—had made Carrie's life a miserable, wretched hell for the past three years. They all hated him, Frankie probably even more than Carrie.

Carrie shot them a hesitant look. "I haven't yet."

Frankie's eyes widened. "What? Why the hell not? That would have been the first thing I would have done."

Again, Carrie gave them a hesitant look and bit her lip. "I haven't told him yet because I'm not entirely sure that I'm going to take it."

There was stunned silence, then... "What?" Frankie asked flatly, as though the idea were ludicrous.

"Why not?" April breathed. She would have thought that Carrie would have jumped at the chance to change jobs.

"Money or principles?" Zora asked.

Carrie snorted. "It's not the money."

Zora nodded thoughtfully.

"Then what's the problem?" Frankie asked, evidently not concerned with principles.

Carrie fiddled with her drink, then cocked her head and offered a strained, almost bitter smile. "They want me to be their *Negligee Gourmet*."

April frowned. "*Negligee Gourmet*," she repeated.

Frankie's lips twisted with knowing humor. "Let me guess—they're angling for the male demographic."

Carrie nodded. "Yep."

"So the premise of the show is you cook wearing sexy nighties?" Zora asked.

"Right again," Carrie told her. "How will anyone ever take me seriously if I do this? Furthermore, if they cancel the show, how will I ever be able to find reputable work again?"

Frankie paused and considered her. "Carrie, there's more to you than a pretty face—you are one helluva chef." She shrugged. "Personally, I think you should take this opportunity and, instead of treating your beauty like a handicap, embrace it. Capitalize on it, babe. Men will watch. Women will envy. Ratings will soar. Even if, God forbid, the show is ever canceled, your talent speaks for itself. Finding a job won't be a problem."

"I agree," Zora added. "It might not be the show you dreamed of, but make it into a new dream."

"Sounds like excellent advice to me," April told Carrie. "Frankly, I'd think anything would be better than working for Martin."

A small smile shaped her lips and a spark of tentative excitement lit her gaze. "There is that."

"Hell, yeah," Frankie said. "Tell him to kiss your sister's black cat's ass and move on."

Carrie paused. "You guys really think I should do it?"

"No question."

"Without a doubt."

"Definitely."

Carrie let go a shaky breath. "Well…all right then."

More whooping laughter and congratulations ensued, once again garnering irritated scowls from other patrons. Annoyed, Frankie raised her arm, evidently prepared to give them the middle finger salute, but thankfully Zora intercepted her hand and forced it back down. "Please," she admonished. "Can't I take you anywhere?"

Disgruntled, Frankie mumbled something uncharitable about rude people, but made no more attempts at sign language.

"All right," Carrie said. "I've shared my good news." Her twinkling gaze slid to April. "That leaves us with you. I understand I'm not the only one who's *experienced* good things this week."

April warmed all over, both at the innuendo and at the reminder. Pleasure still hummed along her nerve endings. "I did."

"Out with it," Frankie demanded impatiently.

April shrugged. "I'm cured."

Zora's mouth curled. "So *The Vagina Whisperer* worked his magic, eh?"

Oy. Had he ever. "Oh, yeah," she told them, inclining her head. "He sure did."

Frankie waited for her to elaborate. "What? No details?"

"She's fixed," Zora chided. "That's good enough for us."

Frankie snorted. "Speak for yourself. If he's got some sexual mojo going on, I need to hear it. It could be good for my column."

Sorry, April thought, but she'd die before she let something as beautiful as what she and Ben shared beneath that tree find its way into Frankie's column. Frankie might have good intentions, but this was private. Special. Cherished. She wasn't prepared to share her breakthrough with the sexually repressed of the world. Was she being stingy? Yes. Because she used to be one of them.

But this was different. It had been way more than sex or making love. She and Ben had connected on a level that she'd never—never—dreamed of, much less experienced. Their souls had mingled. He had surpassed the fantasy, that was for damned sure.

"Well," Carrie said. "The important thing is that you're fixed." She darted April another look. "Is he going to continue to whisper to you, or are you finished with your…treatments?"

April grinned, sliding them all a sly glance. "Oh, I'm not finished. Not by a long shot." In fact, April thought, pulling out her trusty cell, she was due for another one in about, oh, say…fifteen minutes.

9:00 p.m. You're the hunter. I'm the prey. Jackson Square. Find me…then take me.

BEN READ THE DISPLAY twice just to make sure that he hadn't misunderstood, then felt a bolt of heat hit his groin and a broken laugh emerge from his throat.

Damn, but she'd certainly taken to this beck-and-call rule, he thought, feeling the first quickening of excitement zip through his blood. "You're the hunter, I'm the prey," indeed. Now this was a game he could get used to.

Ben checked the time on his cell and decided he had a few minutes to arrange a little preparation of his own. When he found her, he wanted to make sure he had a safe place to *take* her.

Twenty minutes later, he was strolling through the square. Midweek activity was considerably less than weekend, but there was still enough going on that he had to keep a keen eye out for April all the time. Street musicians played moody jazz,

tarot card readers, fortune tellers and the odd artist dotted the city-block-size park.

Rather than wandering aimlessly, he decided to
start at the middle and work his way around. With
that in mind, he made his way to the impressive
statue of Andrew Jackson on horseback—hence
the name *Jackson* Square—that sat in the middle
of the area and scanned the park closely, looking
for anyone who remotely resembled April.

When he didn't readily see her, he went on the
move. He was supposed to be the hunter, after all,
though to be quite honest, he could probably get to
the taking-her part a lot more expediently if he
merely waited. But that was hardly sporting, was it?

He strolled past the Cabildo, Saint Louis Cathe-
dral, and the Presbytere, certain to check amid the
various knots of onlookers stationed in front of each.

Then he moved down the other side, past the
Pontalba buildings, which housed various restau-
rants and specialty shops. She could be in any one
of them, Ben thought, taking his time to carefully
check each storefront and café.

Quite honestly, he expected her to be hiding in
plain sight, otherwise they could be out here all
night, walking in circles around one another. Most
likely she'd chosen one spot to wander around in

and was simply waiting for him to stumble upon it. He found himself walking faster, his heart pounding with an excited thrill-of-the-hunt rhythm that, frankly, he would have never suspected he'd enjoy.

Just knowing that she was here, somewhere in this square waiting for him to find her and take her made the fine hairs on his neck prickle, made his belly clench with lust and his dick swell for sport. Hell, he'd had a friggin' hard-on since the instant he'd read her provocative, wicked instructions.

Quite frankly, bedding her again, sinking into the welcoming heat of her explosively responsive body had consumed every waking—and sleeping—thought since he'd taken her yesterday afternoon. His mind reeled back and visions of pearled nipples and dewy curls, swollen lips and lush breasts filled his thoughts, momentarily blinding him to the sights around him.

God, she'd been perfect. Utterly and completely perfect. Ben had been with countless women, more than he'd had any business bedding. But none of them had ever affected him like April. When he'd slid into her, he'd felt more than his dick engage—he'd felt his heart engage, as well. He was wholly, completely invested in her and had no goal outside of making her want him the way he wanted her. More than desire. More than need. He wanted her to want him. He wanted it to be out of her hands, beyond her control. A mindless surrender that bound her firmly to him.

And after yesterday, he had no intention of ever—*ever*—letting another man have her.

He'd fixed her. She was his.

Now he just had to prove it to her.

Ben's vision returned and he realized he'd unwittingly made his way back around to the Cabildo. And whether good fortune or Providence, a nanosecond later he saw her. A slow, predatory smile spread across his lips. As luck would have it, she was wandering around the very place he'd intended to take her to start with.

How very fortuitous.

He glanced at his watch. They'd be inside the building within three minutes, and he'd be inside her in four.

Moving stealthily, Ben doubled back and blended in with a group of people headed in her direction. As they walked past, he cut from the group, stole up behind her and carefully put his hand over her mouth to prevent her from screaming.

She jumped, but quickly recovered and a muffled laugh sounded against his hand.

"Walk in front of me and do exactly as I say," he told her, playing the hunter role to the hilt. "Follow the alley next to this café around back."

April nodded and set off at a brisk walk, evidently as eager as he was to advance the game.

"There's a back door coming up on the left. Knock once and someone will let us in." She did as he asked, and thankfully, his well-placed call had paid off. The door opened and they were ushered inside a kitchen, heavy with the rich scents of coffee, chicory and beignets. A client of his owned this particular café. It was open twenty-four hours a day and was a local hot spot.

Which made what they were about to do even more fun.

April turned and shot him a questioning glance, awaiting more instructions, he supposed. "I'll take it from here," he told her.

He threaded his fingers through hers, then swiftly led her through the kitchen and into a small hall where a hidden door led to a staircase above the restaurant. Very few people knew about the secret room, which was used to entertain the odd celebrity or city official who longed for a little privacy. It was a parlor of sorts, complete with its own private bath.

When he popped the door open, the look of surprise on her face was priceless. "How did you—"

"Silence," Ben told her. "Prey isn't supposed to question the power of the hunter."

She chuckled and followed him swiftly up the stairs, her feet beating an excited tattoo against the carpeted treads. As per his instructions, a carafe of coffee and order of beignets awaited them.

But they were for later.

The instant April's feet hit the landing, Ben tugged her roughly to him, kissed her hard and started tearing at her clothes, an idea she evidently appreciated because she tore equally as frantically at his.

Shirts flew, pants dropped, a shoe hit the wall, her bra landed on a lamp shade.

Thankfully, underwear was not an issue.

Feeding wildly at her mouth, her breasts, her neck and ears—anywhere he could taste her— Ben lifted her up and backed her against the wall. She wrapped her legs around his waist, her arms around his neck and sighed as his dick nudged her center. He gritted his teeth. She was hot, wet and ready and he wanted her so desperately he thought he'd die if he didn't take her right then.

With a guttural cry that tore from his soul, he buried himself to the hilt inside her. Pumping frantically, he was driven by a need so fierce he could scarcely understand it, much less contain it.

He pistoned in and out of her, her sweet body absorbing his thrusts with a welcoming heat that seeped into his bones. "You make me crazy, you know that?" he asked brokenly.

April laughed. A fine sheen of sweat coated her body and her smile was delighted and satisfied, desperate and starving. "Not as…much as you…make me," she breathed raggedly. "I've been thinking…about you all day. This. You inside me." She closed her eyes, clenched around him. "I can't tell you how good it feels," she said, her voice a keening cry of pleasure. "It's like I'm coming apart inside…and I want to shatter."

He knew exactly what she meant. He wanted to be *with* her—and *in* her—all the time. She was his better half, the yin to his yang…the girl he'd always wanted.

"Oh, God," she said breathlessly, her thighs clamping around him. "It's— I'm—" Her head suddenly became too heavy for her neck and she let it drop forward onto his shoulder. She bit him lightly and tensed as the beginning swirl of climax started sucking her under. He could feel her throbbing around him, getting ready to come. "Oh, sweet heaven," she growled, her voice desperate and husky. "I need— I want—"

Me, Ben silently supplied and, locking his jaw, he pounded into her harder. Her back slid against the wall and she bounced beneath him, riding his dick until he thought his legs would break and his balls would shatter. *Me, dammit. You want me and you're always going to want me because I love you. I've always loved you.*

Her feminine muscles suddenly clamped around him. She stiffened, tightening her legs and met him thrust for thrust.

"Oh, sweet heaven," she growled. "Yes. It's… there!" she screamed, her voice breaking into a loud cry he muffled with his own mouth. He ate that sound, savored it, then before she could finish, he let her down from the wall, and bent her over the nearest chair, driving hard into her from behind.

He wrapped an arm around her waist, slid his hand over her belly and into her curls, then found her hot button. "Hang on, baby. You're in for a bumpy ride."

Then he fingered her clit, pumped deep and fast and hard, could feel his aching balls slapping against her hot, weeping flesh.

She swore. She grunted. She begged. She whimpered. Her breath came in short broken puffs. "Oh, please. *Sonofabitch.* Oh, sweet Jesus, Ben. That's…wicked."

He knew…and that's why she liked it. He'd given her tender. She was due for a little down and dirty.

His legs quaked, his thighs burned and holding himself back had probably caused himself irreparable harm, but he wasn't going to stop until he tore another orgasm from her. She was close, he knew, he could feel her tensing around him with each frantic thrust into her tight heat. He bent down and sank his teeth into the skin where her neck met her shoulder. A light bite, but it did the trick nonetheless.

She broke.

Another stream of inventive obscenities streamed from her lush mouth and she collapsed over the arm of the chair, spent, finished and sated. Three thrusts later, Ben joined her there.

He came. Hard.

So hard in fact that nausea threatened and his

vision blackened around the edges. It took every vestige of strength he had left in his body to maneuver them to the small couch against the wall. He pulled a throw from across the back and draped it over them. Light jazz seeped into the room from outside along with the hum of voices and clanging cutlery through the floor. The scent of coffee, powdered sugar and sex perfumed the air.

Still breathing raggedly, April curled trustingly against him. "You know what?" she asked, her voice rusty from sexual exhaustion.

"What?"

"You just reeled me in." No pretense, no subterfuge, just the good old-fashioned truth.

Ben stilled, felt a tentative smile tug at the corner of his mouth. He was too damned tired to smile. "I did?"

"You did," she murmured. "What about you? Are you reeled in yet?"

He let his head rest against hers and a small chuckle bubbled up from his throat. God, he was tired. "Babe, I've been netted, filleted, battered and fried." His lids drifted shut.

A soft laugh whispered across his chest. "You sound good enough to eat."

Ben's eyes popped open. Surely to God she

didn't mean— He couldn't— Well, he could, he supposed. He'd find the energy somewhere. But—

"Later," she finished weakly, and he fell asleep to the tune of her breathing, safe at last in the arms of her love.

11

"Do you think anyone would notice if we spent the night here?" April asked a couple of hours later. She was still deliciously naked, curled up next to Ben while sampling a beignet and nursing a lukewarm cup of coffee. Surprisingly, it was still good.

"I doubt it," he said, reaching over to wipe what she supposed was powdered sugar from the corner of her mouth. His gaze tangled with hers and he deliberately licked his finger.

Sweet mercy.

He'd wrung her out—taken her against a wall, then bent her over a chair—and yet a single look made another achy twinge tumble in her exhausted loins.

"Why?" he asked. "Do you want to spend the night here?"

"Not necessarily," April told him, swallowing. "I, uh… I just want to spend the night with you."

Falling asleep in his arms a little while ago had been a surprising pleasure. Ordinarily she didn't sleep well with another person in the same bed with her, much less on a cramped little couch. And yet she'd dozed off easily with Ben, had listened to the steady rhythm of his heartbeat beneath her ear. It had been…special. Effortless. Right. Just like everything else between them.

"Well, you can certainly do that," he told her. "My place or yours?"

"Doesn't matter."

"Yours is closer," Ben said.

She nodded. "Then mine it is."

"Is this your way of telling me that we're finished playing hunter?"

April shot him a tired smile. "The prey is exhausted."

"Interesting," Ben said, setting his coffee cup aside. His lips slid into a sexy grin and he helped her stand. "The hunter did all the work."

Feigning outrage, April gaped at him. "*All* the work? I seem to recall a bit of effort on my part."

He shrugged sheepishly. "Okay, maybe not all the work."

She gave an imperious little nod. "Thank you."

Ben slid the pad of his thumb down the side of her face. "You are *most* welcome."

They took turns using the small bath, then dressed and quietly made their way back downstairs. Ben walked her to her car, then she gave him a quick ride to his SUV and he followed her home.

The walk to her door was a quiet one. There was something almost…reverent about this step and it deserved the respect of silence. April inserted her key, flipped the lock and ushered him inside.

While her home wasn't quite as grand as his, it was beautiful nonetheless with a lot of craftsmanship—crown molding, wainscoting and ornate fireplaces and plaster. She'd spent a small fortune having the floors refinished and every bit of the plumbing and electrical had been replaced. She let go a small, expectant breath. But it was home, it was hers, and she loved it.

A firm believer in light therapy, she always left some sort of illumination going, be it a stained glass lamp, or a night-light. A small antique lamp burned on her kitchen counter, giving off a homey glow that warmed her inside.

"This is beautiful, April," Ben said, inspecting

the kitchen. Given the work he'd had done on his own home and the general expertise he had in architecture, she was pleased with his assessment.

"Thanks."

"Did you do the renovations or had they already been done when you bought the house?"

April set her purse down and hung her keys on the hook next to the door. "I did them. What I couldn't manage myself, I had done."

"You've done a helluva job. Would you mind showing me the rest?"

She hadn't expected the request, but given his passion for old things, she wasn't all that surprised, either. "Sure."

She gave him the grand tour—both upstairs and down—then finished up in the living room, her favorite spot in the house. "This room has been a labor of love," she said. She shot him a look. "Some fool put oil-based paint over the fireplace tiles and I had a horrible time getting it off."

Ben quirked a brow. "I can imagine."

She crossed the room and smoothed a hand over the rosewood mantle. "It's taken me a while," she admitted. "I could have mortgaged it and had everything done a lot faster, but I prefer to cover the cost as I go."

His gaze sharpened. "No mortgage?" he asked, seemingly impressed.

April managed a smile. "A combination of savings and trust fund."

He inclined his head knowingly, rubbed the back of his neck and slid her a hesitant glance. "You didn't want to invest your trust fund?"

She chuckled. "You sound like my dad's accountant. He said the same thing. In fact, he almost had a seizure when I refused."

Ben was thoroughly intrigued now. He knew she was smart, obviously had a head for business or couldn't run her own successfully. "Why did you refuse?"

She considered him thoughtfully. "If I tell you, I'll have to break Rule Number Two."

Evidently that was hint enough. He pushed his hands through his hair and stared at her. "Let me guess. Your mother."

April nodded, felt her jaw harden. "My house, my rules. I'll never sell it, I'll never mortgage it," she said matter-of-factly.

A flash of respect kindled in those pale whiskey orbs, making her blush and look away.

"That's certainly easy enough to understand," he said, making his way across the room toward her. Taking her hands and pulling them around his waist, he gazed down at her, with respect and something else, something just beyond her understanding twinkling in those compelling eyes. "You're one shrewd woman, you know that?"

"Thank you," she murmured. "I had sense enough to seek you out, didn't I?"

Ben chuckled. "That you did."

April lowered her voice. "I'm glad you're here."

"I'm glad I'm here, too."

"You ready for bed?"

Ben smiled softly, then hid a yawn behind his fist and followed along behind her. Her bedroom was her sanctuary. Papered in blue toile with crisp white linens and accented in pale yellow, it was soothing yet warm. She'd bought the bedroom suite at an estate sale, one of her favorite pastimes.

Walnut with rosewood inlay, the huge four-poster bed dominated the room and was positioned in a bay window that appeared to have been specifically designed for the frame. The measurements were perfect. The chest of drawers, dresser, highboy and nightstands were all marble topped, ornate and beautiful.

As though they'd been doing this forever rather than for the first time, they readied themselves for bed with surprising ease. April's bathroom was equipped with his and hers vanities and she'd managed to dig out an extra toothbrush from a drawer—a complimentary gift from her last trip to the dentist—for Ben. She listened to his manly sounds as he prepared for bed and felt a keen rush of emotion expand in her chest, pushing a smile on her lips.

They strolled back into her bedroom—he automatically avoided "her" side—and slid beneath the covers. Ben bellied up to her back, slid an arm around her waist and sighed contentedly into her ear. Inexplicably, tears stung the backs of her lids.

"She was wrong," April whispered softly, settling in as a wave of contentedness and joy wrapped her in the swaddling haze of rekindled love. "I won't be sorry."

CAREFUL TO KEEP his breathing even, Ben lay beside April and felt the rest of his body atrophy with dread.

She was wrong. I won't be sorry.

His lips twisted bitterly. He didn't have to guess who the *she* was in that statement. It was horrible that what was obviously one of her mother's dire predictions could infect what should have been the perfect conclusion to the perfect day.

April had all but told him that she was in love with him. They'd had passionate, mind-boggling, soul-sharing sex this evening, then had fallen asleep in each other's arms. Ben swallowed. Tonight he was sharing a bed with the woman he loved and yet, due to Rule Number Two, her vindictive mother and evasive father, he couldn't relax and fully enjoy it.

The lie of omission was there between them, set to tear them apart again if he didn't fess up and tell her the truth.

Or at the very least, make someone else tell her the truth, he thought ominously.

He hadn't spoken to Marcus Wilson in years, so approaching the man now and telling him how to deal with his daughter was probably not going to be met with a warm reception. But he'd be damned before he'd let anything—or anyone—ruin what he and April had rediscovered.

And he knew from experience that her mother wasn't above doing that very thing.

Honestly, the whole damned thing was a powder keg ready to blow. If April found out that he knew about Davy and Marcus's living arrangements and hadn't told her…

Ben mentally swore.

She'd cut him out of her life, Ben thought. Just like she had her mother. Not that he could blame her. Morgana had made her wretched, had controlled every aspect of April's life from the instant she was born, to the instant she left her house. What she wore, what she ate, who she befriended, even who she loved.

Her mother had micromanaged herself right out of April's life, and nothing showcased that fact more than the house he currently slept in.

Rather than investing her trust fund—which in the long run, properly invested, she could have easily tripled—she'd bought a house. And a fantastic house at that, Ben thought. He'd felt the loved and lived-in connection instantly, that same quality that drew him to other old houses, but stronger somehow. April, no doubt. She'd imprinted herself onto it. He could feel her here, as well.

Nevertheless, how many women her age owned their own home, free and clear with no mortgage? Very damned few. Hell, he made an exceedingly comfortable living, but even *he* had a mortgage.

No, she'd been so determined to leave that house—her mother's house, specifically—and never come back that she'd bet it all on a home of her own. *I'll never sell it, I'll never mortgage it.* Powerful words, a powerful woman.

And with every second that ticked by, the lie of omission swelled between them, became more important, more destructive. With every instant that passed, with every emotion that deepened between them, that lie gained momentum.

Nevertheless, anytime he pondered the problem—and he'd circled around it more times than he could conceivably count—he always came back to the same thing. It wasn't his place. Furthermore, how in the hell did you frame the words for that conversation?

April, my dad and your dad are lovers and always have been. My father is the man your father is in love with. Dad wasn't the same after Vietnam and, rather than letting his family suffer, your dad gave him a job and a place to live. He took care of him.

Ben stilled as that last thought registered. He'd never thought about it that way before, he realized, peace coming with the epiphany. And he should have. He should have realized the honor in the act.

Marcus hadn't just conveniently stationed his lover on his property, as Morgana had told him—he'd done it because he loved him. He'd done it to help them—all of them, himself included.

Furthermore, things would have never worked out between his parents even if Marcus hadn't been a factor. Like a lot of gay men of his generation, Ben imagined, his father had tried to do things the PC way. He'd married, even produced a child, but... Oh, well. Water under the bridge.

At any rate, while the new understanding brought comfort, it didn't bring a solution. He was still left with the unhappy task of figuring out what the hell to do. And for whatever reason—instinct, hidden psychic abilities, whatever—he got the distinct impression that time was running out. Morgana had been to see him, had called her daughter and raised immortal hell. She would not sit idly by, not so long as there was a chance she could get her way.

She'd take action. The question was, how would she strike?

Ben lay in the darkness, April's rump pressed deliciously against his groin and waited for some sort of answer to emerge. He'd slung an arm about her waist and could feel the sweet, rhythmic rise and fall of her side beneath him. Her hair spilled over her shoulder, tickling his nose with the scent of her shampoo. He was aware of every breath she breathed, every quiet, sleepy sound that emerged from her lips. She was so soft, he thought. As though she'd been created expressly for him— carved by the same master—she couldn't have fit any more perfectly against him.

He loved her, he thought simply. There was no other explanation for this achy, full feeling in his chest, or the immense, sucking dread the idea of losing her instilled in him. April had always been the one for him, *would* always be the one for him.

And to this day, Ben still carried a vivid memory of when he'd first realized it. Grade school. She'd been in fifth, he'd been in seventh. They'd taken the bus home from school and had been talking about the day—who'd gotten paddled for cheating, who'd gotten caught kissing in the coat closet, average grade-school drama—when all of a sudden she'd gotten this dreamy look on her face and said, "I wouldn't mind getting caught in the coat closet with Jeremy Tillman."

He'd stopped in his tracks. "What?" he'd demanded, because the idea of her going into the coat closet made his belly feel as if he'd eaten a jar of live worms. He'd realized a few minutes later that it wasn't so much her going into the coat closet as her going into it with someone besides him.

She'd shot him a look. "What?" she'd asked, as if he were crazy. "What's wrong with wanting to be kissed? Don't you ever think about it?"

He'd stared at his feet, not knowing what to say. The truth was, until that very moment, he hadn't really thought about it.

But then an odd thing happened—he'd looked at her mouth.

The sweet bow at the center of her upper lip, the plump, rosy bottom…and his insides had knotted, his palms had gotten sticky and his face had flamed.

"I guess," he'd lied. "But you need to stay out of the coat closet with Jeremy Tillman," he'd added belligerently.

"Melanie Garner says he's a good kisser."

"What's she got to compare it to?" Ben had demanded. "Has she been in the coat closet with every boy in the fifth grade?"

"I don't think so…but she's been kissed and that's more than I can say."

Though his legs had turned to noodles and his

mouth to dust, Ben had decided that the best way to keep her from venturing into the coat closet with Jeremy Tillman was to kiss her himself. "Well, if you want to be kissed that bad, I'll kiss you."

She'd darted him a hopeful glance, which had quickly turned to one of curiosity. "I would like to know what the big deal is," she'd said, as though it were merely an experiment.

"Fine. I'll kiss you." He'd taken her hand, waited for her to close her eyes, then with a nervous, shallow breath, he'd pressed his lips to hers. She'd tasted like summer heat and Big Red bubble gum and the bottoms of his feet had gone numb, standing there as the hot May sun had beat down on their heads.

Eyes wide, April had drawn back and tentatively touched her lips. At the time, he'd thought he might have done something wrong—hell, he'd never kissed a girl before—but then a slow smile had slid across her face and she'd said, "Wow...no wonder Melanie spends so much time in the coat closet."

"Yeah, well, you just stay out of there," he'd told her. "The next time you want a kiss, you just come see me."

And she had. Ben smiled, remembering.

That had been the beginning of a romantic relationship that had lasted until her mother had intervened. Which was why he had no intention of letting history repeat itself.

There had to be a way out, had to be a solution. Ben stilled as the inkling of an idea began to form. Maybe he didn't so much have to *tell* her as *show* her, Ben thought.

Bring her by sometime, his father had said. *I'd love to see her...and I suspect someone else would, as well.*

His father had given him the answer, dammit, Ben thought wildly. It had been there all along. Davy had issued the invitation. All Ben had to do was make sure that April accompanied him. Problem solved. Marcus would be forced to tell her— which he should have had the guts to do a long time ago.

Satisfied that he'd discerned a workable solution, Ben pulled her more closely against him. He'd use Rule Number One to get her there. That way, he wouldn't violate Rule Number Two. And after it was over and done with, they could concentrate on Rule Number Three.

Then he fully planned on instituting a Rule

Number Four—no more lonely nights. He wanted to make permanent sleeping arrangements.

As in, they slept with each other exclusively. For the rest of their lives.

12

APRIL LADLED scrambled eggs onto Ben's plate, then added a few slices of bacon and a biscuit. Looking adorably—sexily—rumpled, Ben glanced up at her and smiled. "Thank you. You didn't have to fix me breakfast."

April loaded her own plate and joined him at the kitchen table. She buttered a biscuit. "Well, before you get a big head, I didn't fix it just for you. I always make breakfast. Margo and Joyce will be along shortly."

He inclined his head. "So I'm just reaping the benefit of Margo and Joyce's breakfast, then."

April felt her lips twitch. "Yeah, I guess you could say that."

"If you weren't making breakfast for Margo and Joyce, would you have made breakfast for me?"

She grinned. "Of course. You're a guest in my house. I'd have to feed you something."

Ben chuckled, those whiskey eyes twinkling with perceptive humor. "So long as I know where I stand," he said, heaving a small sigh.

She didn't care so much about where he stood as much as where he'd lain. Last night had been magical, feeling Ben's reassuring presence at her back. The steady beat of his heart, the whisper of his breath against her hair.

April had slept harder than she ever had in her life. Within minutes of feeling that warm body at her back and masculine hand snugged against her belly, she'd drifted off to the land of Nod, and slept until her alarm sounded this morning.

This morning she'd awakened with a smile, a feeling of contentedness and well-being that hadn't been a part of her daily life in so long, it had taken her a few seconds to identify it. Ben did that for her. He had the singular ability to soothe and inflame, to comfort and impassion. He was the itch and the cure, the balm and the fever. She was without a doubt head over heels in love with him.

She cast him a covert glance, watching him idly shovel his breakfast into his mouth while calmly perusing her paper. Given Rule Number Three, he'd gotten up this morning and slipped back into his jeans, but had neglected to button them or don a shirt. She'd seen him naked, of course, but this was the first time she'd been lucid enough—translate: not sex crazed—to really appreciate him.

And she did *appreciate* him.

Toned muscle, smooth skin, crisp masculine hair. His shoulders were broad and well formed and tapered into a chest that could easily grace the cover of any men's magazine. Six-pack abs drew the eye down to a small line of hair that arrowed beneath the snap of his jeans. A treasure trail, April thought, remembering what lay at the end of that line.

She let go a shuddering breath as moisture seeped into her panties, then looked up and caught Ben staring at her with a lazy grin that told her he knew precisely what she'd been thinking...and he liked it.

"Problem?" he asked, blatantly fishing for a compliment, the wretch.

"Not unless you're sporting a defect I haven't discovered yet," she told him. She propped her chin in her hand. "You're one beautiful man, you know that?"

Ben scribbled something on a corner of the paper, tore it off and handed it to her, then leaned over and kissed the tip of her nose. "Not half as beautiful as you are," he said huskily.

"What's this?" she asked, studying the little piece of paper. It looked like an address.

"It's my Rule Number One. I'm giving it to you in advance. Meet me there at six tonight."

She felt her mouth curl into a crooked smile. "Why didn't you just tell me?"

He shrugged, grinning at her. "What's the fun in that?"

April heard a car pull into the driveway. "Button your pants. Sounds like one of my girls is here. I don't want them getting a peek at my prize."

Ben chuckled. "As the lady wishes. I wouldn't want to risk the wrath of the penis voodoo doll."

He'd just fastened the snap when the back door burst open and Morgana, of all people, stormed in.

Stunned, April gaped at her.

Until this very instant, her mother had never stepped foot inside her house. She'd never been invited and wasn't invited now. April always unlocked the kitchen door in the mornings for Margo and Joyce. It was a habit she'd evidently have to rethink in the future.

Her mother's lips twisted with fury. "You're sleeping with him? You let him spend the night?" she screeched.

April calmly set her fork aside. "Who I sleep with is none of your business. This is not your house."

"I don't care whose house it is!" she screamed, breathing heavily, her lips unnaturally white. "You're my daughter and the idea that you would *defile* yourself by sleeping with that, that *mongrel* makes my stomach turn."

Appalled that her mother would speak that way about Ben, much less in front of him, absolutely infuriated her. "Frankly, Morgana, I don't give a damn. You should leave," April said through tightly gritted teeth. "Now."

"I'm not leaving until he does and I want your promise that he won't be back." She flung her hands up wildly, getting more agitated by the second.

"He's not going anywhere and I'll promise no such thing." April swallowed, trying vainly to maintain some semblance of control. "Either leave now, or I'll have you forcibly removed."

That seemed to sober her, but not in the way that April intended. Her mother smiled cruelly, crossed her arms over her chest and glared at Ben as though he were something she'd scrape off the bottom of her shoe. "You'll call the police on me? On your own mother?"

April nodded. "If it comes to that."

Morgana inclined her head. "Oh, I see how far it's come already. Very well," she said, seemingly coming to a decision. She sent Ben a sinister smile. "Did you tell her yet?" she asked him, her voice poisonously sweet.

April felt a curious sickening sensation take root in her belly. *Mark my words. You'll be sorry.*

"Tell me what?" she asked, certain that she really didn't want to know.

"About your father," Morgana sneered. "Has he told you about your father?"

It took every ounce of strength she possessed, but April didn't betray even a flicker of confusion. She wouldn't give her mother the satisfaction. Her entire face might as well have been injected with BOTOX.

"Yes, he has," she lied, giving what she thought was an Oscar-winning performance considering that her brain whirled with unanswered questions. What did Ben know about her father that she didn't? What could he possibly be privy to that she was not? As far as she knew, Ben hadn't spoken to her father in years. Or for that matter, even his own. It didn't make any sense. Rule Number Two… There was a connection, something she knew she should grasp, but didn't. She—

Morgana's face twisted with rage and she whirled on Ben. "You told her! You told her about Davy and Marcus! That wasn't your place, you bleeding little parasite," she snarled, advancing upon him. "*He* was supposed to tell her! He was supposed to tell her so that she would hate him as much as she hates me! You've ruined it! *How dare you?*"

Davy and Marcus? But what did— Realization dawned, embarrassingly late as usual, April thought as the breakfast she'd just eaten threatened to make an encore appearance. Peace shattered. Hope fled.

He'd known. He'd known that their fathers were lovers…and he hadn't told her.

Mark my words. You'll be sorry.

Damn it to hell, April thought as her heart withered, did the bitch always have to be right?

SHE'D EAT GLASS before she'd let her mother know how cut up she was inside, Ben thought, as April's gaze connected with his. But he saw it—and everything inside him chilled at the hopeless look in those clear green eyes.

He'd fucked up.

Though his first inclination was to explain why he hadn't told her, Ben knew at that moment, that the very best thing he could do for April was to play along. The explanation would have to come later. Provided she'd even hear him out.

He shot her mother an insolent glance. "I *dare* because I can," Ben said. "You're only pissed that you didn't get to tell her first."

"I wanted her father to tell her!" she shrieked. "I wanted vindication. I wanted him to have to confess his *perversion* to her. To explain to her why he'd moved his lover onto our property and forced him to live right under my nose for twenty years."

"You could have divorced him," April said, unnaturally still.

Her mother's sharp gaze swung to her. "And risk being an outcast? Unable to satisfy a husband? Do you know how that felt? Do you have any idea? Seeing them together day after day? Seeing *my* husband in love with a *man?*"

Though April did seem to consider it, ultimately she lifted her shoulder in an unsympathetic shrug. "It would have been better than being miserable. But that's what makes you happy. Wallowing in your misery."

"Then you take up with *him*," Morgana continued at April, evidently ignoring the insightful personality trait her daughter had just offered her. "Bad enough I have to lose my husband to Davy Wilson, but my daughter—my own flesh and blood—to his worthless son?" Morgana's gaze sharpened, cutting to Ben. "You're so smug today, aren't you?" she needled. "But you weren't smug when I told you about your father, were you? You weren't smug when you found out that he'd whored himself for a place to live."

April gasped. "You did what?"

Her mother's eyes sparkled with malicious glee. "Didn't tell her that, did you? Ashamed of the truth?"

Ben shook his head. "I'm not ashamed of anything," Ben told her, his voice throbbing with pent-up anger. "Least of all my father. He's a good man."

"Ha! By whose definition? What sort of a man moves his family onto his married lover's estate? A lazy one," she said, her lips twisting with ugliness. "Shiftless."

"Get out," April said, her voice barely understandable through her gritted teeth. "Get out now and never—*never*—come back."

Morgana drew herself up. "You can't talk to me like that. I'm your mo—"

"Not anymore," April said. She stood and advanced, causing her mother to retreat a step. "You're poison. You're cancer. You're bitter…and you are no longer welcome in my life. Leave now."

"But—"

April took another threatening step and her mother wisely retreated. "Fine," she said as she opened the door. "Choose the mongrel. Choose your father. You've never been anything but a disappointment anyway." Then she turned and walked out. The slamming of the door echoed in the silence yawning between them.

April stood with her back to him, ramrod straight and unmoving. "Ben?"

"April, I—"

"Were you going to tell me?"

He couldn't lie to her, even now, when he knew it would save his own skin. "No, I was going to sh—"

She laughed, an it-figured sort of chuckle that made his stomach roll. "Get out."

Ben shoved a hand through his hair. "April, let me—"

"*Get. Out.*"

"That address I gave you, it's—"

"*Get out!*" Her voice broke and he watched her press her fist to her mouth. "Go now."

Arguing was a moot point. He knew it. Could see it in the rigid set of her shoulders, the finality of her voice. She was finished with him. Cutting him out.

It was over. And he'd lost her.

His entire body went numb at the thought. Regret and dread, dashed hopes and broken dreams swirled around inside him until he thought he was going to puke. Nausea clawed its way up the back of his throat.

"My dad asked me to bring you by," he told her. "The address is on the table if you want to see your father."

Then, though every instinct told him to wrap his arms around her to prevent her from shattering, Ben turned to leave. He knew his touch wouldn't be accepted.

Like her mother, he, too, was no longer welcome in her life. He walked outside and retched beside his car.

APRIL WAITED for the door to close behind Ben, then the sob that had been trying to scramble up her throat for the past five minutes broke loose and she cried as though her heart was breaking.

And it was.

How could he have kept something like that from her? she thought, wounded far more than she would have thought possible. She snorted, shook her head. God, sometimes she was such a fool. Even Frankie had figured it out.

And that certainly explained Rule Number Two, she thought with a bitter laugh. No wonder he hadn't wanted to talk about their parents. Their fathers were lovers. Had always been lovers.

It boggled the mind.

April could always remember her father and Davy being good friends, but she'd never noted anything out of the ordinary between them. She knew that her parents' marriage wasn't the best— hell, no one could live with her mother. Naturally on the rare occasions she'd been able to visit a friend's house, she'd noted the difference between other parents and her mother and dad. Other parents were generally affectionate and spoke to each other. Hers didn't. Nevertheless, it had been her perception of normal and she'd never really considered anything beyond getting out of the house herself.

She could see why her mother had stayed with her father—as she'd pointed out earlier, her mother was happiest in her misery. But what possible reason could he have had for staying with Morgana? It didn't make any sense.

April replayed the scene in her kitchen, and though she was angry and hurt at Ben for not telling her about Davy and her dad, she couldn't help but feel her heart prick every time she thought about her mother telling him all those horrible things about his dad. Parasite? Whore? God, the woman was twisted. Bent. That was why he'd stopped seeing her, April realized. Not because of any statutory rape threat, but because her mother had made him ashamed. Her eyes watered. And he'd adored his father.

Her heart broke for him.

As an adult, surely to God he knew better, April thought. Her father had loved Davy, had wanted him close, had wanted to take care of him. There was nothing sinister in that. They'd merely wanted to be together and had worked out the best possible way.

It still didn't explain why her father wouldn't confide in her, though. That hurt. When had she ever given him the impression that his happiness wasn't important to her? That she wouldn't love him unless he was heterosexual? She loved him no matter what. Hell, as long as he was with someone who treated him well, she didn't care who he lived with. Quite frankly, she was thrilled that it was Davy. She'd always thought the world of Ben's dad. She couldn't have picked a better person for her father to love.

April's gaze drifted to the table where Ben's note still lay. *My dad asked me to bring you by sometime. The address is on the table if you want to see your father.*

She frowned. But she'd asked him if he was ever going to tell her and he'd said no. Why then would he take her—

Oh.

He could show her without telling her. That's what he'd meant. April wanted to see the nobility in keeping her father's secret—she truly did because that would give her a reason to forgive Ben—but knowing he'd kept it from her, she couldn't get past the hurt that he'd been able to share her body and her bed, yet not tell her something like this.

No matter how you sliced and diced it, it was wrong. Just plain wrong. Noble…but wrong.

And she was tired of secrets, dammit. She picked up the address and committed it to memory. It was time she and her father had a talk.

13

THIRTY MINUTES LATER, after a quick shower and a pep talk, April was on her father's doorstep. Strangely, she could have walked. He and Davy had made their home less than three blocks from her own.

Looking a little grayer and more heavily wrinkled than when she'd last seen him, Davy answered the door. His surprise quickly morphed into delight and his eyes, ones she recognized all too well—they were remarkably like Ben's—twinkled down at her. "You came," he said approvingly, then looked over her shoulder, evidently looking for Ben.

"Er…he's not with me, I'm afraid."

Davy stilled and those shrewd eyes considered her. "Is something wrong?"

"My mother paid me a visit this morning."

He inclined his head knowingly. "Oh." Evidently that was explanation enough. "Oh, Lord. Look at me leaving you standing on the front porch! Come on in. I'll let your dad know you're here."

April nodded. "Thanks, Davy."

He paused. "For what it's worth, child, I've tried to get him to tell you. I don't know what he's afraid of."

April swallowed as a lump of emotion formed in her throat. "Me either, Davy. I just want him to be happy, and I'm glad that he's found that with you."

He smiled, seemed to wilt a little. "I'd hoped so." He turned toward the back of the house and hollered down the hall. "Marcus, you've got a visitor in the parlor."

She heard footsteps. "A visitor?"

The sound of her father's voice made tears burn the backs of her lids and her stomach twisted into a Celtic knot. Three seconds later, her father appeared in the doorway. He saw her, stopped and blinked as though not quite sure she was real. "April."

"Hi, Daddy."

"I'll leave you to it," Davy said with a warm smile and he quietly left the room.

Her father darted her a questioning glance. "How did you— Who told you—"

"Mother came to see me this morning. She thought Ben had spilled the beans."

Her father passed a hand over his face and sank onto the nearest chair. "He hadn't, had he?"

"No."

"Good," her father said succinctly. "It wasn't his place."

"No," April said, struggling to suppress her irritation. "That would have been yours."

He had the grace to look sheepish. "You're right. I'm sorry."

"Why, Dad?" April asked, struggling to blink back tears. "Why did you think you couldn't tell me? Did you believe I'd think less of you? That I wouldn't love you? What? What possible reason could you have had not to tell me, especially after I saw you last summer?"

Her father hung his head, scrubbed a weary hand over his face. "Honestly? I was afraid you'd take it the same way Ben did when he found out about Davy."

"What do you mean?"

"He's had nothing to do with him," her father said. "Until this past week, he wouldn't even talk to him unless he had to. Birthdays, holidays. It broke my heart watching Davy try over and over, never giving up." He smiled sadly. "You see, everyone thinks he's the weak one and yet I'm the one who lacks courage. I couldn't stand the idea of you doing that to me, of rejecting me over and over. It— It's just too hard."

April walked over, sat down next to her father and took his hand. "Daddy, I would never do that to you." Furthermore, she knew why Ben had taken Davy's secret hard, but evidently neither her father or Davy did. "And I think I can explain why Ben's acted the way he has."

Her father arched a brow. "You can?"

April related everything her mother had spewed out this morning, the whole sordid tale, not sugarcoating any of it. "She made him ashamed, Dad. He's just now learning that there was nothing to be ashamed of."

"That vindictive bitch," Davy said from the doorway, his usually smiling face ashen.

April nodded. "I know."

Marcus and Davy shared a look. "Well, that certainly explains a lot," her father said.

"Yes, it does," Davy remarked thoughtfully. "I've lost ten years with my son because that manipulative harpy couldn't accept that you were gay."

"Why did you stay with her?" April asked. "What reason could you have possibly had?"

Marcus and Davy shared another look, then a sad smile shaped her father's lips. "You, sweetheart. I stayed with her for you."

He couldn't have shocked her more if he'd slapped her. *"What?"* April breathed.

"I thought it would be best."

"Well, it wasn't," she said flatly, unwilling to spare his feelings.

Her father released a regretful sigh. "Hindsight, sweetheart. I'm very sorry."

"No lasting harm done," she said. Her mother might have made her wretched for the first eighteen years of her life, but April still had the remaining seventy-plus, she hoped.

Her father gratefully accepted her grace and then frowned thoughtfully. "How did you find me?"

"I gave Ben our address," Davy said. He cast April an intrigued glance. "But I thought you weren't due to arrive until six."

April blinked. "That's right, but— Wait," she said. "How did you know?"

"I got a message from Ben this morning. He said the two of you would be coming by at six."

Her father's eyes widened. "So that's why you cancelled our dancing lessons, then? Your gout's not acting up?"

Davy grinned. "No. But my son needed me— for a change—and your daughter needs you. I really thought this nonsense had gone on long enough. See, Marcus," Davy said, "I told you that you'd underestimated April."

Her dad smiled. "And we've both evidently underestimated my ex-wife's ability to wound. I'm glad that things are improving with you and Ben."

Davy smiled and cast her a significant look. "Now it seems there's only one relationship that needs to be repaired." He quirked a brow. "You'll be taking care of that, won't you?"

April hesitated, still hurt that Ben hadn't shared this with her. She understood, but still couldn't altogether forgive him.

Davy frowned. "You know he was bringing you over here. Surely you can't still be angry with him for not telling you. It wasn't his place."

So she'd heard, April thought, struggling to make it all square up in her mind.

"Let me ask you something," Davy said instead. "If it had been the other way around, would you have told Ben about me?"

April's first inclination would have been to say yes, but within seconds of really considering the question, she knew that she wouldn't have. As Ben had tried to do, she would have attempted to force Davy's hand. No, he hadn't told her, because he'd felt it was wrong. But he had planned to show her, to fix things, and that she decided was good enough.

April exhaled a breath, felt her heart thaw out once more. "No, I wouldn't have told him."

"Then fix it," Davy told her. "Trust me, the longer you wait, the worse it is."

She nodded, then stood and gave both of them a hug in turn. "I love you, Daddy. Stop avoiding me," she admonished.

"I love you, too, angel," he said, his voice thick with emotion. He kissed her cheek. "And I promise to keep in touch."

"You should. We're practically neighbors."

"I know. I, uh, wanted to be close to you."

"I fix breakfast every morning," she said. "You have a standing invitation."

"Will my son be joining us?" Davy asked shrewdly.

April considered him for a moment. "Actually," she said slowly as a plan began to form, "I won't be home tomorrow morning, but every morning beyond that should be good."

They both nodded, seemingly pleased.

April left with a considerably lighter heart than what she'd arrived with. Thanks to Ben, she had her orgasm *and* her father back.

He'd made her dreams come true. Now it was time to return the favor.

14

WELL, THANKS TO STUPID Rule Number Two, April had been ignoring his repeated attempts to get her to respond to Rule Number One. He'd hoped that after she'd had a chance to calm down, she'd at least want to meet him at six at his father's house. But Ben had driven by a couple of times around the prescribed time and, when he hadn't seen her car, he decided not to stop.

A crappy thing to do to the father he'd just made amends with, but in all honesty, he hardly considered himself any kind of company. He'd been in a foul mood all day—a fact that Claudette had only been too happy to share with him.

"I won't tolerate this sort of abuse," she said, when he hadn't properly thanked her for fetching a batch of negatives—ironically, the very ones that had contained those candids of April he'd shot earlier in the week.

Abuse? Ben had thought. He'd forgotten to thank her—discourteous, yes. But abuse? Hell, it's not like he'd backhanded her.

He scowled. That temptation had been reserved for April's mother. Ben's fists involuntarily clenched, remembering the hurt that woman had single-handedly inflicted over the years…. He didn't think he'd ever hated anyone more.

To be fair, he'd like to blame her for this most recent disaster, but this time, he had to take the blame himself. He should have just told April, dammit. In light of what he'd lost, trumping Marcus would have been worth it.

Anything would have been worth it.

"I'm leaving now," Claudette announced from the doorway.

She used to ask if he needed anything first, he thought sourly. Evidently that nicety had vanished with the "new" her. "Have a good weekend," Ben said all the same.

"You, too." She paused, shot him a concerned look. "Can I get anything for you before I go?" she asked.

Ben felt a tired smile catch the corner of his mouth. Ah, he thought, a glimpse of the old Claudette. Evidently she was learning to blend the two. "No, but thanks for offering."

"You're welcome. Well," she said briskly. "I'm off to a meeting." She turned and started for the door.

Remembering April's rebuke regarding his secretary, Ben looked up. "Wait, Claudette."

She paused, glanced over her shoulder.

"When's your birthday?"

She smiled softly. "January twenty-first."

Ben nodded, jotted it down. "Just asking," he told her. "Er…what sort of meeting are you going to?"

Her smile widened. "I would have thought April would have told you."

He blinked. "April?"

"I joined Chicks In Charge last week," Claudette told him. "That's one helluva girl you've got there, Ben. Don't screw it up."

And with that grave advice ringing in his ears, his secretary turned and walked away. Shocked, Ben sat there and laughed. He *had* seen her wink at April, dammit. And when he'd complained about something "getting into" his help, she'd known exactly what that something was. Her girl-power group. Evidently he hadn't been the only one keeping secrets, though admittedly, his was the greater sin.

Oh, screw it, Ben thought after a few hopelessly unproductive moments. He wasn't going to get any more work done tonight. He could just as easily be morose and miserable at home. He tidied his desk, gathered the negatives of April and headed home.

He needed to get a dog, he decided as he let himself into his empty house. It would be nice to have the companionship, the unfailing love and devotion, someone who'd be happy to see him when he walked through the door.

Anything was better than the silence, the sound of his own thoughts.

He poured a scotch, sank into a chair and channel surfed until he found a ball game. He wasn't much of a sports enthusiast, but he'd heard that this was what men did when they had absolutely nothing else to do.

He didn't know how long he sat there before he dozed off, but the sound of a knock at his back door jolted him awake. He blinked groggily, attempting to pull his thoughts together. The knock sounded again.

Ben passed a hand over his face and tiredly made his way to the back of the house. He opened the door…

And got the shock of his life.

April stood at the threshold. Like his dream come to life, clad in a sheer white gown—with nothing on underneath—she smiled tentatively, took his hand and started leading him through the house.

"What—"

She turned and pressed a finger against his lips, silencing him. She said nothing, just tugged him onward, a vision in moon glow. His dream seductress. She unerringly led him upstairs to his bedroom, whirled him around and backed him toward the four-poster until his knees hit the bed, forcing him to sit down.

She bent and tugged off his shoes, then his pants—in light of Rule Number Three, underwear wasn't a problem—followed by his shirt and tie. She took her time while she undressed him, smoothing her hands over each inch of flesh she exposed, growling her appreciation low in her throat, nonsensical sounds of approval that instantly pushed his dick to attention.

Oh, sweet hell, Ben thought, watching her. It was one of the most erotic things he'd ever seen.

Her seducing *him.*

She pushed him farther up on the bed, backing

him up so that she could scale his body. She left the gown on—a gift in a pretty package—and the fabric was smooth and cool against his skin. His breath stuttered out of his lungs as the first touch of her lips branded his belly. She licked her way up, listening to his own telling sounds. A quick inhalation, a throaty growl. She nipped lightly at his nipple, played at the other with the tip of her nail and unexpected pleasure bolted through him.

She smiled against him, the she-devil, thoroughly enjoying making *his* fantasy come to life. Every move was calculated and sexy and meant to bring him joy. Now that was a novel experience, to say the least. Women had always been more interested in what he could do for them, than the other way around.

That April had listened enough to know what he wanted, then actually forgiven him—he firmly intended to get the skinny on that later—and decided to enact it made Ben's previously morose heart swell equally as rapidly as an important organ south of his navel.

She braced both hands on either side of his face, searched his eyes, letting him see the need, the desire, the regret, but most importantly, the *want*.

She wanted him.

His throat tightened, forcing him to swallow. She waited, making sure that he understood, then slowly lowered her lips and kissed his lids, his cheeks, the side of his neck, then finally his mouth. Slowly at first, tentatively and reverently, then passion flared and she deepened the kiss, moving further into seduction mode. She was above him, dominating him, forcing him to let her take the lead. It terrified and thrilled him, making him shake and burn.

She worked her way back down his body once more, painting a deliberate path down his belly, over his navel. She took him in hand, slid her fingers up and down, gazed at his dick as though it was the tastiest thing she'd ever seen, then bent her head, and, with her gaze connected to his, she took all of him into her mouth.

He'd been wrong, Ben decided. *That* was the most erotic thing he'd ever seen. A guttural growl tore from his throat and his thighs went rigid.

April's eyes finally fluttered shut, a look of sublime satisfaction on her face, and she sucked and licked, nibbled and stroked until his coming in her mouth was going to be a foregone conclusion if she didn't stop soon. He could feel the climax building, the impending orgasm a loaded bullet ready to shoot down the barrel of a gun.

She mewled around him, made happy noises of pleasure that vibrated against his throbbing dick. "I love the way you feel in my mouth," she said, her voice a sleepy-sounding purr. "Soft, hard and salty."

Her hand cupped his balls, dallied languidly while she increased the hungry slip and slide of her mouth.

"April," he growled, "unless you want this to be over in a few seconds, babe, you're going to have to stop."

She sucked him harder, her lips curling into a smile around his dick. "Now that would be a pity. Because I'm not nearly finished with you yet."

She licked a pearl of desire from his engorged head, then licked her lips. "You'd said that you'd been netted, filleted, battered and fried," she told him, her eyes gleaming with wicked humor. "Now you've been eaten."

He chuckled, he couldn't help himself. Here he was about to detonate like a bomb and she had the presence of mind to crack a joke. Something was wrong with this picture.

She scaled his body once more and abruptly

straddled him, her weeping flesh settling firmly onto his rod.

Ben abruptly stopped laughing.

Her eyes rolled back in her head and she winced with pleasure at the intimate connection. "Do you know how many times I've thought about this?" she asked him.

She rocked against him, purposely dragging her wet folds over him, coating him with her warmth.

"How many times I've lain in my bed and thought about having you in this very position. Beneath me. At my mercy."

He shook his head, mesmerized.

"Hundreds, thousands probably. See," she said, "the thing is, I've been in love with you since I was sixteen."

She lifted her hips, guided him to her center, then impaled herself on him. Ben locked his jaw, felt the breath rush out of his lungs.

"And I'm still in love with you."

He flexed beneath her, anchoring his hands on her hips, and winced as she started to ride him. Up down, up down, a soft undulation, a promise, a prayer.

She loved him.

He bent forward and captured her nipple through the fabric, felt a corresponding clench around his dick and sucked harder. A maelstrom of feeling commenced in his body. His heart ached, his dick throbbed and he was suddenly hit with the extremely unusual urge to scream. Or weep. He didn't know.

She loved him.

She braced her hands upon his chest, rode him harder, her lush breasts jiggling as she absorbed the force of his thrusts. He could feel her clamping against him as though reluctant to let him leave, but just as anxious for the return. She bit her lip and her eyes fluttered shut. Her head lolled to the side, her neck seemingly too weak to support it any longer. Her breath came in little jagged puffs and a fine sheen of sweat had broken out on her forehead.

She was beautiful, a sexual goddess, his fantasy come to life. She was everything. His world. His past. His future…

And she loved him.

Without warning, he came hard, felt the orgasm tear from his loins and blast into her. His lips peeled back from his teeth, his neck bowed off the bed and a long keening groan issued from his throat.

Three seconds later, April joined him there. She bent forward, locked her legs and pumped frantically against him, pushing his dick against her G-spot, dragging her clit along his skin.

Suddenly she tensed, her mouth opened in a silent wail and she shuddered violently atop him. He felt her feminine muscles close around him, causing even more spasms of pleasure to issue out of his loins.

With a soft supplicating sigh that whispered around his heart, April collapsed on top of him, her hair spilling over his chest, the gown bunching beneath her.

Ben ran his hands over her rump, drawing figure eights up her back. "I love you, too," he said simply. "It's always been you, April."

She leaned up and her gaze searched his. "I'm sorry for not listening to you today. I should have. You were trying to tell me and I—"

Ben shook his head. "Forget it. I should have told you. I just—"

"Couldn't," she finished. "I know. I don't blame you. It wasn't your place. It was my dad's." She smiled softly. "I went and talked to him today," she said.

Ben smiled. "You did?"

"Yeah, after you left. I couldn't wait until six. I had too many questions."

That was certainly understandable, Ben thought. He'd had a decade to deal with the idea of their fathers being lovers. She'd had less than twelve hours. "And was everything answered to your satisfaction?"

"Yes." She bit her lip, hesitated. "Why didn't you ever tell anybody what my mother had said to you, Ben? You know she's a vindictive bitch."

"I asked my mother about it and she left," he said, shrugging in an offhand manner that in no way matched the way he felt. "I didn't want to risk it."

Her gaze softened, misted. "Oh, Ben. Your dad loves you. Surely you know that?"

He did now. He nodded, finding it too difficult to speak.

She smiled down at him. "You're pretty damned lovable."

His heart did another little flip and he grinned at her. "So are you." His gaze traced the wonderfully familiar curves of her face. "Last night, I was thinking about our rules and I think we need to amend one of them."

She arched a brow. "Oh? Which one?"

"I think we need to do away with Rule Number Two completely."

She nodded, her green eyes twinkling. "I am in total agreement with you. Rule Number Two sucked."

"And I'd like to propose a new one." His belly quivered with nerves.

"And what would that one be?"

Ben reached up and tucked her hair behind her ear. "One of the till-death-do-us-part variety."

A slow dawning smile eased wonderingly across her lips and her eyes misted again. "I'm in total agreement with that one, as well."

"Will you marry me?"

She sank her teeth into her bottom lip and nodded. Tears sparkled on her lashes. "Definitely."

"And we'll live at your house," he said, willing to give up his own in order to make her happy. He'd give up everything to make her happy. Besides, he'd felt the magic there. They'd make a beautiful life together in that house, making love and raising babies.

A half laugh, half cry rushed past her lips. "Oh, Ben."

"So long as we can play the hunter and prey game," he stipulated. "That was pretty damned fun."

She giggled, bent forward and kissed him softly. And, for some reason, he was reminded of that first kiss, their first commingled breath, the one that had sealed this very end all those years ago.

"No more playing in the coat closet for you," he said playfully.

She chuckled, her breasts vibrating against his ever expanding chest. "And no more *whispering* for you." She arched an imperious brow. "I've got a penis voodoo doll and I'm not afraid to use it."

Epilogue

"YOU KNOW, I'M REALLY starting to get pissed off," Frankie said. "*I* get engaged and *you* get married."

April grinned. "There's the pastor," she told her friend, gesturing toward the portly man-of-the-church who'd just married them. "Do something about it."

Frankie shook her dark head. "Nah, we're waiting. We've still got lots of plans to make."

"See," April told her. "That's where you messed up. You should have never agreed to let him make any plans. Straight men don't know how to plan a wedding."

"Well, not everybody can have the fab gay duo in their corner," Frankie said with a fond smile as she stared across the reception room at April's dad and Davy.

There was that, April thought. The two of them

had been in cake-and-lace heaven since she and Ben had announced their engagement. They had insisted on planning the wedding. Since that freed her and Ben up to make the most out of Rules One and Three, she didn't mind.

Just last night *she'd* been the hunter and *he'd* been the prey. Talk about thrilling stuff, April thought, scanning the crowded room for her sexy new husband. She spotted him in the corner talking with Ross and Tate, and from the looks of things they were—vainly—trying to give her new hubby the proper instruction for the care and feeding of a Chick In Charge.

Let'em try, April thought. She and Ben had their own system and she figured as long as neither one of them ever wore underwear, they'd do just fine.

Looking slightly nauseated but beautiful all the same, Zora strolled up. "Please don't have stargazer lilies at your wedding, Frankie."

April winced. "Sorry. Are they making you ill?"

"Positively wretched. But not to worry. According to my husband, I should stop being affected by scents within the month."

Frankie smiled, crossed her arms over her chest. "He's taking his daddy duties seriously, isn't he?"

"You know Tate," Zora said, gazing fondly at her husband. "He doesn't do anything in half measures."

Frankie snorted. "It would serve him right if this baby was a girl."

Zora chuckled. "Believe me, that has been discussed at length."

Carrie picked through the crowd and gave April a warm hug. "Congratulations, April. I'm so happy for you." She looked at Zora. "What's been discussed at length?" she asked, jumping into the conversation.

"The poetic justice of my husband dealing with a daughter."

Carrie chuckled knowingly. "Oh, yeah. That would be perfect."

"We'll see, I guess," Zora said.

"When's your ultrasound?" Frankie asked.

"In a couple of months."

"Are you going to find out the sex of the baby?" April asked.

She knew lots of parents did, but she wasn't so certain she'd want to when she and Ben started a family. Which, according to him, would be soon. He'd told her that he was looking forward to inseminating the hell out of her as quickly as possible. The fathers were anxious for grandbabies, and truthfully, she was feeling distinctly envious of Zora at the moment.

Zora shook her head. "No, I don't think so."

"You'll change your mind," Frankie predicted. "You know how you are. You'll want to decorate the nursery and buy clothes and you'll *have* to know."

While that was an accurate assessment of Zora's Type-A character, marriage had mellowed her some. "We'll see," her friend said. She glanced at Carrie. "How are things down at the set?"

"All right, I guess," Carrie said, somewhat evasively. "The powers that be want to pair me up with Philip Mallory—"

"That insufferable Brit with the nice ass?" Frankie interrupted.

Carrie nodded. "One and the same."

"For what?" April asked.

"Some sort of special. I don't have any specifics on it right now."

"Keep us posted," Frankie said. She frowned

thoughtfully. "I've always had a thing for a British accent. Very sexy."

Carrie let go a small breath, but didn't comment, which piqued April's interest. Hmm, she wondered. Was there some cookin' going on after the show? Evidently Zora had picked up on Carrie's odd behavior, as well, and she and April shared a look.

Very interesting, April thought.

A telltale buzz from her cell phone started against her thigh beneath her garter and a shot of excitement bolted through her. She'd been waiting for this message. "Form a circle around me," she said impatiently. "Hurry. Quick. Move, move, move."

Bewildered, her friends huddled around her as she fumbled with her dress.

"What the hell are you—" Frankie inhaled sharply. "You're wearing your cell phone beneath your dress? Have you lost your mind?"

April peered at the display and grinned. Nope. Just her heart.

Coat closet. Now.

She gathered her dress and bolted away from them. "Gotta go," she called over her shoulder. "My honeymoon awaits."

"B-but the car is that way," Carrie told her, looking hopelessly confused.

But her groom was this way, April thought. Waiting for her. With no underwear on.

* * * * *

But wait…it's not over yet!
Don't miss Carrie's story, GETTING IT NOW!
Available next month. Things are
really heating up…